KALPAR

Silas & Bundersnoot

To Peabody, who always asked, "But has Bundersnoot been fed?"

Contents

Acknowledgement

Original credit for this book, or perhaps blame, must go first and foremost to my friend Austin and his wife Lauren. It was May of 2020, all of us were stuck at home, and I was casting about for new writing ideas. They suggested the idea of a retired adventuring sorcerer who owned a shop with a bodega cat and they used their experience to help people with various magical problems. *Silas & Bundersnoot* is the result of that idea.

Thanks goes to Isabella Betita, my editor, who was extremely excited to work with me on this project and said it was cozy fantasy in all the best way. Also to my cover artist, George Patsouras, who managed to bring these guys to life.

Among my personal circle I want to personally thank: My librarian friend Bridgid, who described me as one of the best writers she knew and was consistently excited for this project to come to fruition. My therapist, Dr. Macha, who thought it was so cool that I had this goal and encouraged me every step of the way. Everyone in Laser the Boy's discord who saw me write Silas and Bundersnoot as part of our Thing a Week challenge. I don't know your real names, but your heart reacts brought my joy. And everyone else I actually knew who promised to buy a copy when it finally released. There are so many of you.

Finally, and most importantly, to my loving spouse Peabody who let me engage in this ridiculous vanity project.

On Werewolves

The young man looked at the shop, consulted the scrap of paper in his hand, and looked at the shop again. Basking in the sunlight, Bundersnoot watched the young man through the front window. He estimated the man would spend another two minutes before either entering the shop to ask if it was the right place or leaving in defeat. It probably would have helped if the shop had a sign but that was the entire point: if Silas had put a sign up over the shop then all manner of people would be coming in night and day asking for silly things they thought magic could give them. This way, only the people who really, truly *needed* the help of a wizard would be able to find him.

Bundersnoot stretched and leapt down from the window, negotiating the cluttered floor of the shop, although cluttered wasn't quite the right word for it. It was wholly inadequate to describe the state the shop was in. Between the wood shop counter and the door was a small clear space where the admittedly few customers could enter. Any progress further into the shop involved navigating the narrow canyons between mounds of items. Piles of clothing, varying in quality from embroidered finery fresh from the seamstress to tattered rags fit only to make paper, formed a lumpy mountain range. A labyrinth of shelves held glass jars filled with everything from dried flowers to crushed stones to more exotic ingredients labeled "dreams" or "memories". Most impressive of all was the collection of books: tattered manuscripts barely held together with string, scrolls made from papyrus, hand-written codices representing lifetimes of effort, and most rare of all beautiful leather-bound tomes fresh from the printers' district. Silas knew every item in his shop and exactly where it was.

The bronze bell above the door jangled and Bundersnoot jumped onto the shop counter. "Silas, we have a visitor!" Then he turned and faced the young man who'd finally gathered enough courage to enter the shop. "Silas will be with you in a moment, he's bringing me food."

"Uh—I guess I'm in the right place?" The young man's confusion was understandable. While many people spoke to their cats, having the cat reply was a far rarer occurrence. "I mean, a wizard would have a talking cat, yes?"

"Yes, although if he did anything other than lie all day I might find him actually useful." Silas emerged from behind a curtain that separated presumably the back room from the rest of the shop. Silas was a man of indeterminate age. His hair and beard were white, but his face maintained a youthful vitality with none of the typical marks of age. However it was the clothes, a simple robe of deep crimson, which made it obvious that Silas was a wizard. For whatever reason once wizards reached a certain level of skill they decided that a robe was all they ever needed to wear in life ever again. "I'm not feeding you, Bundersnoot, you just ate."

"Yes, and I can see the bottom of my bowl again. Clearly the food needs to be refreshed." Bundersnoot flopped on his belly and looked mournfully at the young man. "I'll waste away to nothing at this rate. It's a disgrace is what it is."

Silas ignored this comment and turned to the young man. "How can I help you today?"

"It's about my sister," the young man said. "It's —well—you see… She's been turned into a werewolf."

Silas and Bundersnoot exchanged the look of two experienced professionals. "Young man, you've certainly come to the right place," Silas said. "Based on the fact that you're here rather than in the Temple District speaking with the Dragonslayer Guild you must be hoping to affect a cure for your sister's condition?"

"Yes, sir. —You see my sister Erica, she's been in charge of our ropeworks ever since our ma died two years ago. She's all that our da has left and if she dies without a daughter our ropeworks will go to our aunt. And she's never much cared for our da, thought our ma was too good for him and, well that's all family politics." The young man gave the grim smile survivors of bitter family fights were all too familiar with.

Silas took out a notebook and a quill pen. "I'm going to need some details of the accident first. What's your name?"

"Claude, Claude Cordeur. Of the Cordeur Rope Works."

"Very good." Silas recognized the name. The Courdeurs were a long-established artisan family of the city of Elade-voc. Not prosperous enough to play the game of city politics, but still industrious and respectable. What can you tell me about how your sister became a werewolf?"

"Last month she went up into the hills to take a look at one of the tar kilns we'd been getting supplies from, she weren't satisfied with the supplies they'd been sending us, you see."

"Anyway, so she went up to have a talk with our suppliers. And one night there was an attack at the camp. Wolves came out of nowhere and started attacking everyone in the camp.

The next day it looked like—well—they said it looked like she were dead, sir. Just straight dead. But when the moon came out the next night…she was fine. Stood up and started walking around."

"And then the next night?"

"The next night…They said she turned into a wolf."

"They said? You didn't see it yourself?"

"No, sir. She was still up in the hills. Erica, she didn't have any memory of it. Just said she had the strangest dreams. But the men—They said such awful stories. That she ripped out the throat of the foreman and dragged his body into the woods. The next morning there was nothing but bones left. And me da and me, we talked about getting a Dragonslayer. We— weren't proud of that discussion."

"But Erica owns our ropeworks in her own right, ever since our ma died. And if she died then it'd pass to our aunt and me da and me, we'd be out on the streets. But even then—I don't think we could." Claude shuddered, his cloth hat bunched in his hands. He paused for a moment, taking a deep breath, and then looked at Silas with tears in his eyes. "Me da and me, we love Erica. If there's even a chance that we could cure her, we couldn't let that pass us by. So please, sir, can you help?"

Silas nibbled on the end of the quill and consulted his notes. "Well, young Master Cordeur, from what you told me I suspect that your sister has one of the simpler versions of lycanthropy. If we wanted to simply treat the condition there are a number of things we could do. Tinctures made from wolf's bane are capable of preventing transformation at the full moon, although you have to take it regularly and there are mixed results. If you don't make the tincture correctly you can poison the patient. Alternately we can look into keeping her contained during the transformation but that is fairly resource intensive and there's a risk she might break out."

"Is there a more—permanent solution?" Claude asked.

"Other than a silvered blade? Not terribly likely." Bundersnoot said and Silas shushed him with a hand.

"The next full moon is in three days," Silas said. "Come back the day after tomorrow with your father and if there's even a possibility of curing her affliction we'll make an attempt. If not, we'll treat your sister's condition." Claude looked crestfallen. "Cheer up, young man, there are plenty of people who live perfectly happy lives with lycanthropy. We'll figure something out."

* * *

"I'm telling you, Silas, it can't be done! It's impossible to reverse the werewolf's curse! Now when are you going to climb down from there and feed me?" Bundersnoot pranced around the base of a ladder propped against one of the bookshelves in Silas's shop.

Silas looked down from his perch on the book shelf, at a height much greater than the exterior of the shop should have allowed. "I fed you not two hours ago."

"Well how long ago is that? I am starving!"

"Recent enough that if I fed you again you're liable to explode, you horrid little glutton." Silas sighed and turned back to his books, running his finger across the spines. "Let's see, Foglio referenced Hus. Hus referenced D'Quay. D'Quay referenced Servicus who is somewhere…"

"But if you fed me you could accomplish something actually useful opposed to looking for a cure that doesn't exist!"

"Ah! Servicus's *Journeys Beyond the Desert*." Silas carefully removed a tome from the stack and with a cry of triumph slid down the ladder. "You're only saying it's impossible to cure a werewolf because it's never been done."

"Precisely! Because it's impossible."

Silas squatted down and rubbed Bundersnoot's chin. "Bundersnoot, what if I was to tell you about a little place far south, beyond the Nebian Desert, where they actually discovered a cure for a werewolf?"

"I'd say I don't believe you." Bundersnoot started purring with pleasure and then batted at Silas's hand. "Stop that, you're trying to distract me."

"You really ought to read more, Bundersnoot, it'd distract you from your desire to become approximately spherical. Then you'd know about a story— a story based on a myth, a myth based on a legend, and a legend based on a history. And if Servicus is correct, and he was correct about a great many other things, then we may have a cure."

* * *

Claude had returned with his father on the appointed day. The elder Cordeur had streaks of silver shot through his black hair and was heavily tanned from his work outdoors. His well-muscled body spoke to a lifetime spent at physical labor. Silas ushered them into one of the many, many back rooms of his shop.

"The cure is fairly simple but I cannot do it alone. I will need your help in performing the cure and cannot guarantee your safety." The two men tried to sink further into the overstuffed armchairs. "I'm not going to lie to you, so I want you to fully understand the werewolf's curse and the risk you're placing yourselves in. According to Claude's story Erica was wounded by a wolf, transformed, and killed while in the wolf shape. This is the most common version of lycanthropy and I have seen multiple cases in my years as an adventurer.

"In every instance the curse compels the victim to hunt their closest kin until none remain. Isolated and outcast, the victim becomes the curse's thrall and seeks only to spread it as far as possible. I will do everything that I can to try to protect you, but there will be considerable danger to both of you. The three nights of the full moon begin tomorrow night. If we are going to attempt a cure, I need both of you to agree right now, without reservation."

Claude and his father looked at each other, the fear obvious in both their faces. "Please, sir, I'll do whatever it takes to get me Erica back," the father said. "That's all I want."

Silas turned to Claude and he gave a firm nod of assent. "Whatever it takes, sir. We'll do it."

"All right, here's what we're going to do."

* * *

There was a howl outside the house, a spine-tingling sound that bypassed the human mind entirely and told the monkey brain that it was dinnertime and they were on the menu. Both Claude and his father gripped the silver amulets Silas had given them until the metal bent under the pressure. Silas did his best to project a cool aura of calm and confidence as he added the finishing touches to the magic circle he had chalked out on the floor of the Cordeur home. The key thing was projecting, because internally Silas was just as terrified as the Courdeur men. The last time he had fought a werewolf it was with the protection of several armed men; Silas wasn't certain his magics alone would be able to protect them.

"Is this going to work?" Claude asked.

"It's too late to be having second thoughts at this point," Bundersnoot said. "Silas, there's a bit to your left that needs a touch more wolf's bane." Silas bent down and sprinkled powdered herb into the spot Bundernoot indicated with his paw. "Circle's complete, get everything you want to keep inside because I'm closing it now." Silas carefully stepped into the circle and joined Bundersnoot, who began to glow green with magical energy. There was an audible *snap* as the energy began to thrum into the circle. It is a well known principle that cats can channel magic which is why so many practitioners kept them as familiars.

"Is it normal to feel your back teeth tingling?" Claude asked.

"Just for the first few minutes," Silas responded, "but don't worry, we're going to have a whole lot to distract us soon!"

There was another howl and the scrape of claws against the door of the house. The door itself was a solid three inches of oak, banded with bronze. It seemed improbable that even a werewolf could break through that formidable barrier, but Silas had seen a lot of improbable things happen in his lifetime. There was a loud thud and the door rattled in its frame. Only the stout hinges and the heavy reinforced bar kept the door from bursting under the creature's assault. Then there were more tentative scrapings at the door before then the creature went silent, as if it had walked off.

"Is that it? Is she…" Silas shushed the father before he could say anything stupid. Suddenly there was another terrible howl outside and the wolf thudded at the shutters.

"Oh no," Claude whispered. "Oh no, I forgot to lock the shutters on the second floor. How high can a wolf jump?"

"Regular wolf? Probably not high enough to break through a window," Bundersnoot said confidently. This was immediately followed by the sound of shattering of wood and glass from upstairs. "But this presents no problem for werewolves, apparently! Everybody get ready!" There was another deafening howl, loud enough to rattle the rafters above them, and the panting of a hungry beast closing in on its prey.

The stairs creaked as the werewolf stalked its way down to the main floor, its claws scraping on the polished wood. Claude and his father huddled together towards the center of the circle. While Silas made sure there were no breaks in the magic protecting them all. The first anyone saw of it was the red glow of its eyes in the shadows. Slowly, menacingly, the brown-furred creature stepped into the candlelight, stalking towards its prey. To all appearances the wolf appeared to be perfectly normal, half as tall as a grown man and weighing just as much. But anyone who looked into the eyes of a werewolf would see the human intelligence, no animal was capable of such cruelty.

The wolf padded to within a few feet of the circle's edge and stopped, sniffing the air then it whuffed with frustration and began to follow the perimeter of the circle. It eyed Claude and his father maliciously, the blood-red tongue slavering over wicked, sharp, ivory teeth.

Finding no break in the circle or Bundersnoot's power, the werewolf lifted its nose into the air and, with visible confusion, took another deep breath. "She's noticed it," Silas said, "everyone get ready." The werewolf cautiously approached a bundle of clothing on the floor and gave it a very deep sniff.

She blinked in confusion. "Now!"

"E-Erica. You need to put your clothes on." The werewolf looked up and gave Claude and his father a critical eye. But it pawed at the bundle of clothing and gave it another sniff.

"Erica! Put your clothes on!" Claude shouted, growing with confidence as Bundersnoot's circle held. The werewolf flinched this time and whimpered in confusion, backing away from the clothing. Carefully, she padded around the circle and scrabbled at the bar on the door, trying to escape from the house. The werewolf's prodigious strength let it shift the bar slightly, but its lack of hands defeated its efforts. The werewolf began eyeing the shuttered windows of the house.

"Quick, before she gets out!" Silas said.

"Erica Cordeur, you put your clothes back on right now, godsdamnit!" the elder Cordeur snapped with the mingled frustration and fear of a parent desperately trying to help their child. The werewolf whined as it drew back towards the clothes. When it reached the clothing it started to—morph; that was the only word to describe it. As she drew the clothing onto her body she shifted, losing the fur, the fangs, the claws, turning back into a perfectly normal person.

"Erica!" Claude and his father both rushed towards her but were stopped when the edge of the circle flashed a bright, unearthly green. They turned to Silas.

"Hold on," Silas warned, "Give her a minute to adjust."

Erica stared at her hands and then touched her face, checking her body. She had a puzzled expression, unable to understand her good fortune. "I'm back? I'm…I'm not a wolf? Daddy? Claude? Oh gods, are you both okay?"

"Bundersnoot, I think we can drop the circle now." Bundersnoot nodded and with a *crack* the green light surrounding the cat went out and everyone could feel the air whooshing out from inside the circle. Claude and his father rushed forward and embraced Erica.

"Erica, we were so worried!"

"We thought we'd never see you again!"

"I thought I'd killed you!" Erica sobbed with relief and embraced her family.

This happy family reunion continued for some minutes before Silas delicately cleared his throat. The family turned to face him, their faces filled with joy, relief, and—ultimately—love. The elder Cordeur stepped forward, his face streaming with tears. "Thank you, sir. We thought it couldn't be done, but you brought our Erica back. Please, we haven't much, but whatever you ask."

"What you owe me will, in fact, be very little. You might even think it merely a token payment. But rest assured, the knowledge I have gained this night has far more value than you could every guess." Silas began returning magical equipment to his satchel. "However, I believe we may be speaking prematurely of recompense. There are still two nights of the full moon and I will not know if the curse has been completely broken. In fact, we may never know for certain. All that being said the initial results are…rather promising."

* * *

"Well, it's been three months now and no signs of Erica changing. It certainly looks like the curse has been broken." Silas grunted in assent and Bundersnoot flicked his tail in irritation. He got up and casually trotted on top of the book Silas was reading and plopped himself across it. "You didn't really know that cure would work, did you?"

"If you mean, was I absolutely certain that it would work the first time without fail? No, I wasn't. But I had a feeling that it would."

"Oh that is a load of nonsense. Back in your adventuring days your party would never let you try something like that without a detailed explanation. Hell, Gerald would have *demanded* you write a detailed report of the potential outcomes and survival probabilities."

"There you go again." Silas rolled his eyes. "Gerald couldn't read, much less understand the concept of probabilities."

"All right, Narses, then."

"Narses, I'll grant you. A more obstinate old fart I've yet to meet."

"You're avoiding my question, Silas. What made you think that particular cure would work."

"Aside from the fact the story had the ring of truth about it?"

"Yes! Aside from that! Gods, you can be so obtuse."

"Well that's easy, Bundersnoot," Silas said, booping the cat on his nose. "Everyone knows true love is the best way to break a curse."

On Fairies

"We don't do love potions!" Silas cried from atop a ladder in the upper reaches of his shop. The little bell over the door alerted him that someone had entered his shop so he started making his way down, books balanced in one hand. "No potions, amulets, charms, or talismans. I don't know if the hedge witch is still over in North Gate but I heard favorable reviews. Well, until she turned that watchman into a pig." Ever since he had helped the Cordeur family word had spread that Silas the Wizard could work miracles. Unfortunately this led to an endless stream of forlorn young people coming into his shop and interrupting his *important* research. Bundersnoot had even given up his favorite sunny spot to escape the onslaught.

Silas was about halfway down the ladder when he finally caught sight of the customer. The first thing he noticed was how terribly *young* she was, although that was almost a relative term for a wizard of Silas's age. She couldn't have been more than sixteen or seventeen if she was a day. Her clothes were travel-stained and ragged, typical of the peasants who lived in the farmlands which fed the great city of Elade-voc. She looked up nervously. "Is this the shop of Silas the Wizard?"

Silas groaned internally and almost wished she *was* a lovestruck youth looking for some magic. Only incredible need could have driven someone this young and this poor to make the journey to his shop. "Yes. I'm terribly sorry, young miss, you caught me at a bad moment. I'll be with you in a minute. Bundersnoot, where are you? We have a customer."

The girl looked around and gave a small yelp when a marmalade-colored cat jumped down from one of the piles of magical ingredients and walked over to her. She was even more startled when the cat started talking. "Greetings, young miss. I am Bundersnoot, familiar of the dread and powerful wizard Silas, master of the eight schools, traveler to the four and twenty planes. I don't suppose you have any treats for a deserving feline such as myself."

"Bundersnoot!" Silas gave an exasperated cry. "I swear to the gods and the Empress when I get down there…"

"I. Am. Starving," Bundersnoot protested, looking up at Silas. "It's been—at *least* six hours since you've fed me."

"You poor creature," Silas's voice dripped with sarcasm. "Pay him no heed, he's always trying to trick people into feeding him." Silas finally reached the bottom of the ladder and carefully placed the books on the counter. "How can we help you today?"

"My name's Adeline, and I've come because," Adeline paused, biting her lip nervously. "I think my daughter's a Changeling."

Bundersnoot hissed and Silas made a gesture against misfortune, something he as a wizard knew perfectly well would have no effect in keeping away the attention of the Fae but had been ingrained as habit by his peasant father. "That *is* unusual, there haven't been Fae this far from Tevioch in, what?"

"Hundred years at least," Bundersnoot said. "Closer to two I think."

Silas nodded. "Miss Adeline, I can see you've come a terribly long way and you wouldn't seek us out if your need was not great. I shall have to ask you some difficult questions but please, let us show you some hospitality." Silas raised a portion of the counter and walked to the door, locking it and drawing the blinds. He headed back to the curtains behind the counter and beckoned for Adeline to follow, but she hesitated, uncertain about following Silas deeper into his shop. "You have my oath as a wizard no harm shall befall you while you are within these walls."

Like all wizard residences, Silas's shop contained far more within its walls than the outer footprint of the building would suggest. This certainly cannot be ascribed to cheapness on the part of wizards because the labor and materials involved in creating extra spaces often far exceed building in the conventional manner. In fact wizards choose extra-dimensional construction for a number of reasons: the ability to maintain a low profile with a perfectly ordinary home which does not immediately scream "WIZARD" to the entire population; the ability to rearrange their residence to suit their own tastes and needs including the ability to add an additional laboratory or storage room as needs arise. But most importantly because wizards are invariably ornery curmudgeons who would rather go through the aggravation of bending space and time by themselves than talk to craftspeople to *build* another room when they need one.

Eventually they arrived in a room that was part laboratory but mostly kitchen. Silas invited the hesitant Adeline to sit at a large wooden farm table in one of the functional but not uncomfortable chairs. Bundersnoot jumped up and curled in her lap, purring contentedly. Without a second thought Adeline started petting him, timidly at first but with growing confidence.

Silas ignited a fire with a simple cantrip, summoning a small flame of wytchfyre in his hand and using it to light the kindling, before putting the kettle on to make tea. He took a seat across from her at the table and pulled a notebook and quill pen from the pockets of his robes. "How about you start with when you first thought your daughter was replaced by a Changeling."

"I think it was two months ago. I didn't notice at first because she'd just started teething so I assumed that's why she cried all the time. But after a few days I thought something was….odd. My husband's mother just thought it was nerves, this being our first baby and all. And then her teeth started coming in and they were wrong." Adeline stopped petting Bundersnoot and stared at the surface of the table, unable to make eye contact with Silas.

"Wrong? Wrong how?"

"There were too many of them, thirty at least, and all of them were sharp like a cat's teeth. We didn't know what to think so we took her to the village wise woman. She was the first to say that it was a Changeling."

"And what did you think?"

"I didn't want to believe it at first. I screamed, I cried, and for two weeks I didn't talk to anyone. But then I started to notice other things that were wrong. Her mouth was too wide, her eyes would change colors, her limbs started to grow strangely. I was sad, I was angry, I was a hundred different emotions at once. But I knew one thing: I wanted to know who had taken my baby and I wanted her back."

"Is there anywhere near your village that the elders always tell people to stay away from? A certain glade, a barrow, a hidden pool, anything like that?" In his adventuring days Silas had tangled with the Fae only a handful of times. But in every case the Fae entered the human world through a place where the fabric between worlds was thin. If her daughter had been replaced by a Changeling they most likely would need to go into the Land of the Fae to retrieve her — which was his biggest concern.

"There are some standing stones near our village that have been there for ages. The wise woman always tells us to stay away from it, but nobody takes her seriously. A lot of us young people find it a convenient spot for…some privacy." She blushed slightly but started when Bundersnoot hissed.

"Standing stones, I might have known. That will be it, Silas, I'll eat my tail if I'm wrong. And you can bet the energy all those young people are expending is the honey that's luring in the flies. We might need help for this one."

"Please, Master Silas." There were tears in Adeline's eyes. "I don't have much but I'll do anything to get my baby back. Please. Anything you ask. Just—please."

There was a long moment as Silas mustered his thoughts. "Miss Adeline, I will offer you some advice. A less scrupulous wizard would take advantage of a statement made in emotional distress. One of the Fae would definitely take advantage. Fortunately for you, I am a man of some—not many but some— principles. If your child was taken two months ago I fear we will not have much time to rescue her, the Fae tire quickly of children. Bundersnoot and I shall need to make preparations but we can take you back home tomorrow." Silas got up and pulled the kettle off the fire. "In the meantime, please try to get some rest."

Adeline rubbed the tears from her eyes and sniffled. "Thank you, Master Silas, a thousand times thank you."

* * *

"No doubt about it, this is a Gate and it's still open." Silas could hear the capital letter in Bundersnoot's voice as they looked at the collection of standing stones. It wasn't much to look at, just a few mehnirs erected in a rough circle all of them overgrown with moss. Most people would have called them elf stones or a fairy ring, but Silas and Bundersnoot were both experienced enough to know there were certain words you didn't speak. They might attract unwanted—attention. "I don't suppose…" Bundersnoot flicked his tail nervously and circled a standing stone warily. "You don't think it's one of *Hers* do you?"

There was only one person Her referred to, could only refer to because there was one name you *never* invoked near a Gate, that of the Departed Empress Allie. Empress Allie was a figure from the dawn of history, because Her arrival had made all history before Her irrelevant. With Her elven armies, legions of sorcerers, and mastery of the elements She had conquered a continent and ruled Amastica for over three hundred years before departing with Her elven armies back into the Land of the Fae.

In the seven hundred years since then the Amastican Empire had diminished but Allie's very human descendants still ruled from Tevioch, far across the mountains to the west. There were entire religions built up around the Empress's eventual return and while it seemed far-fetched—you never knew if She was still listening.

Silas carefully touched one of the mehnirs and scraped some moss away. "No, this is too old to be one of Hers. Much, much too old." The cleared surface of the stone revealed a strangely fluid writing that seemed to move as you read it. "This text is nothing like Old Amastican, and I don't see any unicorns or phoenixes. This dates *well* before Her arrival. I suspect She may not have even known it was here. If the texts are to be believed, She was always very possessive of who could travel between here and…-There."

"Or whoever built this Gate was strong enough to stand up to Her."

"Now there's a chilling thought. Come on, let's get away from here. I think these stones are listening far more than I like." Silas and Bundersnoot left the circle of standing stones, following the narrow dirt trace through the forest back to the village. "I wish we had more time to do research. If I knew whose Gate this was I could better prepare."

"I don't know, Silas, someone from this far back might not even *have* a name. Or it's been forgotten." The emerged from the woods, blinking in the sunlight, and entered the village. Like most farming villages surrounding Elade-voc, Twoforks was oriented along one central dirt road with houses on either side. The homes were small and simple but carefully maintained by their owners. Most of the villagers were going about their daily tasks and exchanging gossip but their suspicion of outsiders meant they all gave Silas a wide berth as he walked by. Adeline and her family were the only villagers who interacted with him, waiting expectantly outside their home.

Aware that time was short, Silas got straight to business. "We found the Gate, but if we're going to rescue your daughter we need to move quickly. We'll have to go through the Gate, you and me, Adeline. And there's a very good chance we won't make it back. Are you prepared to risk that?"

Adeline nodded, resolute, "Yes. Whatever it takes."

"All right. Now Bundersnoot and I can't actually open the

Gate, not without possibly bringing something worse through so we'll have to make somebody else do it for us. Take me to the Changeling."

Adeline led them to a small outbuilding that in better times had probably held livestock. She removed the heavy wood beam that had been drawn across the door and pulled it open. Sunlight entered the building through the open door and gaps in the building's siding, but the interior remained dusky dim and in the darkest corner was a figure small enough Silas could have easily put it in his cauldron."Back again, are we?" There was an ungodly cackle that sounded like a throttled chicken. "I've been so lonely mama. Why do you keep me in this shed, mama? Why?"

Adeline was about to give a bitter response, but Silas raised a hand. "Silence, creature, we've enough of your falsehoods. By the eight schools I ask you: What business did your mistress send you here on?"

There was a sharp intake of breath and the Changeling shrank away from Silas. "Wizzzarrrddd." The word was drawn out in a hiss. "We did not foresee such a development. My mistress shall be most displeased."

Silas entered the shed and loomed over the Fae. "I'm in no mood to bandy words with you, Changeling, so I'll ask you again: What is your business here?" The creature may have resembled a human child at one point, but now its unearthly origins was clear. The teeth were far too sharp, the ears came to delicate points, and the arms and legs were thin, disproportionate sticks with absolutely no baby fat.

The Changeling laughed again, a brutal animal sound. "You cannot compel me to talk, Wizard. Your power is *nothing* compared to the wroth of my mistress. There is nothing you can do to me that she cannot do a thousand ways worse."

"We'll see about that." Silas pulled a small bag out of his robes and poured some black flakes into his hand. "Do you know what this is?"

The Changeling sniffed the air and its eyes went wide with shock. "The Nemesis? You bring the Nemesis in here? You wouldn't dare, wizard!"

"Wouldn't I?" Silas asked rhetorically and threw the flakes at the Changeling. Green wytchfyre broke out over the Changeling's body. It screamed in pain and it scrabbled at the walls of the shed, trying to get away from Silas, but the shed had been built to keep even clever livestock from escaping. The wytchfyre did not spread to the dry wood of the shed but stubbornly clung to the Changeling's body, releasing a harsh metallic smell as it burned. Finally it rolled on the ground to extinguish the flames.

"What was that?" Adeline asked.

"Hammerscale, it's a rare ingredient I got from one of my contacts in the lands across the sea. Apparently it's just waste for them, a byproduct of making iron."

"Iron? What's that?"

"The Nemesis! The Foe-Metal! Bound to serve man and harm us!" The Changeling had extinguished the flames and was standing again. "That was a wicked, evil thing you brought, Wizard! A curse be upon-" Whatever the Changeling was about to say was cut off as it received another face full of hammerscale.

"I'm rapidly loosing patience, creature." Silas reached into the bag and held a few flakes in his hand threatening. "I've already asked twice, I shan't ask again. What is your business?"

"Food!" the Changeling gasped. Its skin was blackened and charred where the hammerscale had touched it, but already the skin was healing. "We needed food. The Queen needed a human child to sustain her power. So they sent me."

Silas cursed. "Bundersnoot, get in here! Adeline, we're going to get your daughter back, I just hope that we can get there in time to save her."

The Changeling laughed again. "You think you can just break through the Gate? No mortal power can command the Gates, wizard! You'll never…"

"That's why *you* are going to open the Gate for us, Changeling."

"No! You can't! I won't!"

"You can and you will." There was a low growl as Bundersnoot padded into the shed. Bundersnoot normally appeared as a pampered shop cat, interested in little more than naps and his next meal, but now that soft, spoiled creature was gone, replaced with a deadly predator. "I have gotten quite hungry, Faeling, and you look like a *very* hearty meal."

The Changeling stepped back, its eyes wide with fear, but it remained defiant. "Her Majesty will do unspeakable things to me if I should fail her. I would rather die first."

"We'll see about that," Bundersnoot purred and without warning pounced towards the Changeling. This proved too much for the Changeling's self-composure. It screamed in panic as it ran the small confines of the shed, Bundersnoot chasing but never quite catching it. The Changeling darted towards the still-open door of the shed and fled into the sunlight, never wondering why Bundersnoot had given it a chance at all.

"Come on, after them!" Silas and Adeline ran after the pair, through the single lane of the village and into the woods. The Changeling kept trying to escape, breaking in one direction and then another, attempting to disappear into the undergrowth of the forest, but Bundersnoot always seemed to be one step ahead, always herding the Changeling back towards the Gate. Even as Adeline stumbled, struggling to keep up in her rough wooden clogs, Bundersnoot kept the Changeling from getting too far ahead. When they arrived at the Gate, Bundersnoot had the Changeling cornered, pinned between two of the stones.

"Nowhere else to run, Changeling," Bundersnoot growled. "Best open that Gate up."

"I don't have to!" The Changeling gasped, but it struggled for breath. It looked—thin, like a piece of cloth that had been worn, rubbed, and used until it was just on the edge of getting holes in it. "I can…I can still run in this world. You'll get tired eventually."

"Perhaps. But how long will your magic hold out?" Silas poured some more hammerscale into his hand. "That was a neat trick, recovering from the iron like that but it had to take a toll, didn't it? Frankly, I'd be surprised if you could still open the Gate at this point, you look fairly spent. I suppose I'll have to settle for the satisfaction of killing you."

Before Silas could move the Changeling screamed and made a circular gesture with its arms. With a crack like wood being split, a green oval appeared behind the Changeling, between two of the standing stones, perhaps only a yard high. The Changeling easily jumped through the Gate and, just as quickly as it appeared, it started to close.

"Silas, now!" Bundersnoot yelled. He looked like he was straining to hold something with his mouth, his tail erect and straight as a ruler. Silas stepped forward behind Bundersnoot, dropping the hammerscale and muttering words of power. He strained his arms like a man struggling to force a door open. Slowly, slowly the portal stopped shrinking and gradually began to grow. When it was finally large enough for Silas and Adeline to pass through Silas stopped.

"Bundersnoot, do you have it anchored?"

Bundersnoot sat down and let out a breath, relaxing his grimace. "Yes. I can keep this Gate open but I don't know for how long. An hour? Maybe two? And that doesn't even factor in time dilation."

"We'll have to risk it." Silas bent down and picked up his sack of hammerscale, returning it to his pocket. He turned to Adeline and extended a hand. "Last chance to turn back."

Nervous but determined, Adeline took Silas's hand. "Let's get my baby back."

"Good luck to both of you!" Bundersnoot called as Silas and Adeline jumped through the Gate. There was a sensation of falling, but much like falling in a dream—there was no sense of danger at the end, just endless height. Then there was a sudden stop and they landed in the sensation of cold. The sort of cold that came on a winter night when the wind cuts through even the thickest of clothing and makes a person want nothing more than huddle around a fire until spring comes again. Eventually the other senses caught up and revealed they were surrounded by towering fir trees, the snow deep around them. Adeline coughed and pushed herself up, brushing snow off her dress. "Where are we?"

Silas stood up, adjusting his belt and going through his pockets and pouches. "Based on the snow and the cold, I would suspect we are in the realm of the Winter Queen."

"The Winter Queen? You mean Giv-"

Silas had covered Adeline's mouth with his hand before she could finish the name, terror evident in his face. "Listen and listen very carefully. Names have power in this place, terrible power. Whatever you do, avoid using names at all. Do you understand?" Adeline nodded hesitantly and Silas slowly removed his hand. "That's the first rule about dealing with this place. The second is do not trust anything. This may look like home but it is a shallow imitation at best." Silas pointed up and Adeline looked at the sky.

The sky was deep black, the sort of black that you only got on the coldest, longest nights of the year in the dead middle of winter. At first it looked normal, like any of the winters Adeline had experienced. But after a moment she gasped, "The stars...There are no stars. And the moon." She turned around, looking back and forth, scanning the horizon. "There's nothing there. Not even clouds. Just blackness."

"Exactly. An imitation of our world but imperfect and incorrect. Do not trust anything here."

"But where do we go now?"

Silas pointed towards a series of small footprints heading away from the glade. "If I had to guess that right there is the trail of breadcrumbs laid for us to follow. Come on, let's get moving." Silas and Adeline started their trudge through the forest. The trail of the Changeling zig-zagged, going first one direction and then another. Regardless of whatever way they were facing, the wind managed to blow directly into their faces, cutting through their rather light clothing and reducing visibility with constantly swirling snow.

Hours could have passed, or days, the lack of stars and moon gave no indication of how long they had been following the still-clear footprints of the Changeling. If Silas hadn't been certain that the trail was deliberate bait before, the fact that it remained untouched despite snow continuing to fall only confirmed this fact. Silas did not like the idea of deliberately walking into a trap.

Silas was a wizard with decades of experience under his belt. He had faced down renegade wizards, followers of insane gods, and even the occasional dragon. But he had never fought one of the Fae on her home territory where the land itself could be used against him. It was sheer lunacy to go charging into a Fae realm when at any moment the Winter Queen could crush them with little more than a thought. And yet—

And yet there was Adeline, a girl younger than Silas had been when he went on his first adventure, who had already done so much to save her daughter. She had left her village, the only world she knew, to ask for help from a wizard. She was pushing onward, despite the wind and snow, scared but determined to see this through to the end. It was amazing what simple love for another could make even the meekest of people do.

With no warning they suddenly found themselves on the banks of a frozen river which split around an island. At the center of the island was a palace constructed entirely from ice, a collection of blues, greens, whites, and hints of purple. A regal but treacherous looking ice bridge connected their bank of the river with the island.

"It's beautiful," Adeline whispered.

"That's a palace of the Fae, and no mistake, your baby will be there."

Light seemed to shine from within the palace, coruscating in rainbow hues. Arches held up with impossibly thin columns of ice buttressed every wall of the structure. But as they came closer the beauty was eclipsed by pervasive menace. The very tops of the walls of the palace were decorated with leering grotesques, ugly and terrifying creatures from the realm of Nightmare, twice as high as a man.

They crossed the bridge and were about to enter the gates when their way was blocked by two hulking trolls. They were unlike the trolls Silas had encountered in the lands around Elade-voc, which rarely topped more than eight or ten feet tall and always looked vaguely like fungus in a humanoid form; these were nearly twice as tall and looked like they were carved from pure stone. With an ominous scraping sound the trolls advanced and formed an impenetrable wall.

"What do we do now?" Adeline whispered, staring up at the gatekeepers.

"You have to issue them a challenge, tell them why you've come and what you want. I don't think getting in will be our problem."

"But what should I say?"

"Just tell the truth and say whatever comes into your mind. The heart will know what to say."

Adeline nodded and walked towards the trolls, who looked down at her. One opened its mouth and there was a sound like a landslide, rocks cascading off each other; it took considerable effort to recognize it as speech. "Who are ye and what business have ye with the Winter Queen?"

Adeline flinched under the auditory assault but stared defiantly at the trolls. "I'm Adeline, daughter of Fabienne, of the village of Twoforks. The Queen took my daughter, and I've come to get her back."

"And your companion?"

"Silas. Wizard." Silas's response was curt and the trolls seemed satisfied with his response. For another eternity the trolls said nothing and remained motionless, leaving no space to pass onto the bridge. Adeline was about to speak again when the rumble of the troll's voice began again.

"Ye have been granted an audience." There was a loud scraping of stone as the trolls stepped aside, paying no further notice to Adeline and Silas as they entered the palace

The entry hall to the Queen's palace was truly immense. Adeline's entire village could have been stored inside it and there would have been plenty of room leftover. The vault of the ceiling disappeared high overhead in a blue-green darkness, and even the echoes of their footsteps seemed swallowed by the depths of the hall.

The walls of the chamber were covered in sculptures twice as tall as a man, all of them depicting the Wild Hunt, that terror from *before* the Empress arrived spoken of only in whispers. Trolls could be seen flaying humans alive in gory detail. Chains of enslaved humans were marched through Gates under the watchful eyes of elven warriors mounted on unnatural steeds. Smaller pixies, brownies, and hobs tormented humans with every cruel device a human torturer ever dreamed of, and a few that they hadn't. Otherwise the entryway was empty, forbidding, and uninviting.

Eventually, they reached an arched entry that led into another massive chamber. Where the atrium was cold and empty, this room was teeming with creatures. Galleries stacked one atop the other stretched beyond the limits of sight, all of them packed with the residents of Fae. Massive trolls stood next to diminutive pixies. Almost-human elves, their bloodthirsty steeds, and monstrous griffins competed for space. Further off weirder, less comprehensible creatures filled out the ranks. And in the center of the room, at the end of a blood red carpet, sat the Queen.

Her throne, like everything in the palace, was designed to intimidate and overawe. The dais alone was as tall as some of the trolls in the room, made from glittering purple ice, each step high and wide enough to make humans struggle to climb it. The throne itself was made from the skull of a leviathan, perhaps one of the mighty ice dragons said to still live far to the north, a testament to her power. The Queen was unearthly, her body all sharp angles like jagged ice. Her skin was a pale blue-white and her flowing hair was shaded a barely noticeable green. A crown made of glittering icicles banded in silver rested upon her brow. Some might call her beautiful but everyone would call her dangerous.

Silas knew from hard experience that nothing with the Fae was ever as it seemed. The Queen's beauty was merely the camouflage of a predator, designed to lure in the unwary until there was no chance of their escape. He respected that danger but also knew that she was the sort of predator you couldn't show weakness to. Then he looked at Adeline and smiled. The Fae weren't the only ones who were more than they initially appeared.

"Remember, Adeline, the heart will know," Silas whispered and gave her a confident smile. "Be brave. For your daughter."

Adeline climbed the first step of the dais to address the Queen who looked at her and deigned to speak. "Who comes before me and my court?" Her tone was languid, almost soporific in its effect, a deep cold that made a person want to crawl under a thick blanket and fall asleep.

Adeline took a breath and then shouted. "You know damn well who I am and why I've come! I've come for my daughter. Where is she?"

"Your daughter?" the Queen giggled and leaned back into her throne. "But Adeline, you didn't want her before. I thought I'd do you a favor and take her for my own. Why should I return her now?"

"How can you say that? She's my daughter! I would never…"

"You thought it in your heart of hearts, my dear." The Queen gave out a malicious chuckle as Adeline paled. "Oh my, yes, I can see into your mind, little human. All your thoughts, your dreams, your desires. Even the ones, no, *especially* the ones you fear to tell anyone else. Your most hidden, forbidden, *shameful* secrets?"

"I saw you that day, little mortal, when you were down by the riverside. You were doing the washing with your baby. She screamed then, she screamed and screamed till her little lungs were fit to burst and in that moment you made a wish. You wished she was gone far, far away from you. I just granted your wish."

"I was tired! I was angry! I hadn't slept in three days! I wasn't thinking straight! You had no right to take her!" Adeline trembled but stared defiantly at the Queen, her fists clenched at her sides in outrage. Silas was unsurprised by the Queen's version of the story. The Fae often preyed on the unaware, granting wishes to advance their own abstruse agendas. Or in this case, taking a resource they needed under false pretenses.

"Tsk, mortals. Always getting upset when their wishes are fulfilled. Never anticipating the consequences. Still, perhaps I wasn't generous with the terms of our bargain. All right, mortal, how about we make a deal? I'll grant you anything your heart desires. You want wealth? I shall give you a queen's ransom. True love? I'll make the most handsome man in the world your devoted slave. Power? I'll give you the secrets of magic only I know. All this and more can be yours and I'll even take my Changeling back. Just give me your child."

"No." Adeline's response was barely a whisper.

The Queen bit her lip, her hand clenching the arm of her throne. "I will only offer one more time, child. Whatever you most desire, speak it now and it shall be yours, and all you need do is let me keep your child."

"No. I want my child back."

The Queen looked like she was about to throw a fit, but some modicum of self-control remained. She sighed dramatically. "Very well, I suppose you leave me no choice you shall have your daughter back." The Queen paused, waiting for Adeline to look hopeful. "Once you pass a final test."

"And what sort of test would this be, Your Majesty?" Silas asked, stepping forward. "Shall she wear out seven pairs of bronze shoes? Sort four types of grain in a night? Bring you a peach of immortality from…Her garden?"

"Oh, nothing so dramatic as that." The Queen laughed Although but Silas noticed her wincing at the mention of Her and smirked. The Queen clapped her hands and two identical children were brought forth by two elvish retainers. "One of these children is your daughter, the other the Changeling. Whichever child you choose shall return with you to the mortal realm. Choose correctly and you shall have your daughter back. Furthermore I shall promise I and my Court shall never again enter the mortal realm to harass you or your kin ever again. But if you choose incorrectly…" The Queen paused as she smiled lasciviously, her tongue skimming across her teeth. "Choose incorrectly and the Changeling shall torment you for the remainder of your pitiful mortal days. Your suffering shall be exquisite and I shall feast on it for quite some time."

"That hardly seems fair," Silas interjected. "Isn't the loss of a child punishment enough?"

The Queen's eyes narrowed and she appraised Silas. "This is

my realm, mortal, and I make the rules. I've already been more than generous." She turned to Adeline. "Choose."

Adeline stared at the two children and turned towards Silas. "How do I choose?"

Silas thought back to the Cordeurs and smiled. "Your heart will know."

"SILENCE!" The Queen screamed and ice flowed out of the floor and encased Silas, entombing him up to his nose. "She must make this decision by herself, unaided by the likes of you, meddling Wizard!"

The cold permeated his very core. The ice made it impossible for him to move even a finger and if he stayed like this much longer Silas had no doubt that he would soon be dead. And yet, despite all this Silas was optimistic. After all, he had true love on his side, how could he possibly lose? Adeline looked between the two children and paused, clearly taking her time to think. She closed her eyes and although Silas couldn't hear her he saw her lips move as she whispered to herself. Eventually Adeline pointed at the child at the Queen's left. "That one. That's my daughter."

"Are you certain?" The Queen smiled maliciously. "You can change your choice…"'

"No. I'm certain." Adeline cut the Queen off and stepped forward to pick up the child. "This one is my daughter." The child immediately gave a baby giggle and grabbed at Adeline, a baby clearly reunited with their parent.

"Fine," The Queen snapped, frowning with disappointment. "This is fine. Fine. I suppose you are…free to return to the mortal realm. You have my word that I will not attempt to harm you or otherwise prevent your return to the mortal realm. Take your wizard and get out of my sight." With a wave of her hand, the Queen dissolved the ice surrounding Silas. He gasped, warmth flooding back into his body as the ice retreated.

"One final thing, Your Majesty," Silas said, unable to resist the need score the final touch.

"What now, wizard? Have I not given everything I promised?"

"You have, Your Majesty, and I have no complaints. But if you were tempted to, say, —renege on certain aspects of this deal it would go quite badly for you. By Your leave" Silas bowed, the model of restrained courtesy, and followed after Adeline and her daughter.

"Who's mama's brave little warrior? Is it you? Is it you?" Adeline tickled her daughter and the baby continued to giggle with obvious enjoyment. "Oh, my little Sylvie, I was so afraid. But your mama's here now, I'm never going to let you be taken away from me. Never again."

"As touching as this family reunion is"—Adeline glared at Silas—"and I *am* touched, genuinely. From the depths of my heart. However, we may want to pick up the pace a little." Silas nodded behind them, where several elves and a few of the— indescribable thing—had broken off from the throng of the court and were following at a discreet distance.

"But the Queen gave her word we would return unharmed."

"Important point about negotiating with the Fae, they are extremely precise in their wording. Her Majesty said she and her court would not enter the mortal realm. However there is an entire court of Fae who now have an opportunity to court favor with their monarch by killing us *and* bringing your child back to her *before* we reach the Gate."

Adeline paled in fear, clutching Sylvie closer to her chest. "What do we do?"

"For now, nothing. I am—*fairly* confident that they won't

attack us within the palace. That would certainly violate the spirit of our agreement. Outside the palace is a different matter."

"What are we going to do?"

"Just keep walking. Don't look nervous or scared, they feed off of that. Just walk. Eyes ahead, confident. Happy you have your baby back."

The walk through the cavernous entry hall seemed to stretch on for forever, the distant gate growing no larger as they approached. Silas suspected some glamour was at work to distort perception in the place, but he didn't have time to analyze it. He was keeping count of the number of Fae following them, mostly elves but a handful of lesser Fae like hobs and at least two of the…things. Silas lost track at thirty. Finally, finally, they emerged into the black night of the outside world. Of the troll guards who had stood here previously there was no trace. "All right, we're going to cross the bridge nice and easy, but when I tell you to run, you start running. Got it?" Adeline nodded in assent.

They were halfway across the bridge when a ululating war cry rose up behind them. Silas looked back and a host of elves, mounted on twisted mockeries of horses, charged forward. "RUN!" Silas shouted but didn't bother to see if Adeline had even followed his directions. Within moments the pouch of hammerscale was in his hand. "Let's hope this works," he muttered as he scattered hammerscale across the bridge, the little pellets of clinking on the ice. Within seconds green wytchfyre sparked around each flake of iron, burning with the intensity of a smelting furnace.

For a moment it looked as if the elves were planning to merely jump over the flames and continue their relentless pursuit of the humans. But there was a mighty *crack* and the bridge split, the magical ice cut through by the nullifying power of the hammerscale. Silas backed away as the center of the bridge collapsed, massive chunks of ice crashing into the river below. The elves reined in their mounts, desperately trying to stop, but claws scrabbled for purchase on the ice and several tumbled over the edge. Those that remained screamed in frustration and shook their weapons at Silas as he retreated. He was certain there was another way for them to cross the river but it would probably take time.

They stumbled through the forest for what could have been hours or minutes, following their tracks back to the Gate. All Adeline could focus on was putting one foot in front of the other as the cold sapped her strength, making it so tempting to just lie down and fall asleep. Silas kept helping her along, attempting what magic he could to help keep them warm but even the most basic spells were an effort of will.

Silas was a wizard at the pinnacle of his craft, a master at tapping the elemental energies which powered all magic. Thanks to years of training he was fairly certain he could summon wytchfyre in his sleep. Only the most difficult and strenuous spells required him to truly focus on the energies and control their flow. But here in the Fae realm those same energies slithered away from him, refusing to cooperate like they did in the mortal world.

Eventually the Gate was within sight, half a mile away at the top of a snowy rise. Adeline seemed to gain a second wind and lifted her daughter up to see the green portal. "Look, Sylvie, we're almost home. We'll be safe and warm." It was at that point that a familiar, keening war cry went up from the woods.

"Sounds like they found a way across the river after all, RUN!" Silas and Adeline scrambled up the hill, stumbling from the cold and the snow but always clawing their way back up and further up the hill. The screams grew closer so Silas risked a look backwards. The elves were visible now, rapidly gaining ground on the two. "Go on ahead! I've got one or two things left I can try."

Adeline nodded continued up the hill as Silas turned fully towards the oncoming Fae. He poured out the last of his hammerscale into his palm, waiting as an elf charged towards him on their mount. When the elf was about to skewer him with their wicked bronze lance he dodged to one side, throwing the hammerscale in the direction of the elf. There was an unearthly scream as both the elf and their mount burst into wytchfyre, the green flames spreading to even the snow. Eventually the hammerscale's power was expended and the flames grew no larger, but continued to burn with an eerie green light. And still the elves came.

Silas could count at least twenty, none of them pausing as they charged forward. He rummaged through his belt pouches until he pulled out a black lump of rock, cool to the touch. "Time to find out if the legends about void iron are true," he said and lifted the stone over his head before throwing it at the ground with full force.

Even before the Empress, humans had known that iron was antithetical to magic and would badly harm creatures for whom magic was fundamental to their existence. The effect of the hammerscale on the Changeling, on the elf and their mount, had been dramatic but understandable. The void iron was orders of magnitude greater.

There was a flash of green light, strong enough to temporarily blind Silas, and heat intense enough to make the Winter Queen's realm feel like high summer. A wall of air pushed outwards and hurled him head over heels. He was no longer sure *where* he was in relation to anything as he was buffeted by wind, heat, and light. It was only through an effort of will that he managed to remain conscious, pushing himself up from the ground when he finally stopped moving, landing in a fortuitously soft snowbank.

Silas managed to get to his feet and surveyed the damage. At the epicenter the world had seemingly ceased to exist, replaced with a black void with only the faintest specks of starlight. Reality looked like a ripped edge of a tapestry, coming loose and fraying at the seams. As Silas watched he realized the void actually was growing and he could see individual strands coming undone. On the opposite edge members of the Queen's court were fleeing, some still tumbling, screaming into the endless void.

"By the Emp-" Silas whispered before catching himself. All the accounts he had found of void iron only spoke of how it acted in the mortal realm. As far as he knew *nobody* had used void iron in the Fae realm, or at least lived to tell about it and it was easy to see why. Whether through divine providence or sheer stupid luck, Silas had somehow survived an outburst of magic capable of punching a hole through the world's fabric. But perhaps even this devastation might prove beneficial, discouraging the Fae from utilizing the Gate due to its proximity.

The Gate was only a few feet away from him and Adeline and Sylvie were safely on the other side, back in the mortal world. Silas had no interest in finding out what mysteries the void contained and walked back through the portal's green light. There was a sensation this time of getting pulled upwards, this time like the sensation of flying rather than falling in a dream. Silas had flown a couple of times using his magic but this bore absolutely no resemblance to that. With a stumble Silas fell and arrived back into the mortal realm.

"Bundersnoot! Sever the link!" Bundersnoot blinked, twitched his whiskers, and the green light of the Gate snapped off as abruptly as a door being slammed closed. "Adeline, Sylvie, did they…"

"Perfectly safe," Bundersnoot purred and with a flick of his tail pointed where Adeline sat, nursing her daughter. "Any chance you're being followed?"

"Um, not *immediately*, no. It will take some time to explain."

"Oh good, you can tell me as you feed me."

* * *

"And heave!" Silas led the villagers in pulling on the rope lashed around the last standing stone. It had taken them three days and ignoring almost every task that needed to be done in the village, but they were pulling the last standing stone out of the ground. Silas was thankful that these stones weren't much bigger than a fully grown human so they didn't have to dig down far to destabilize the stone. The last finally came free of the earth like a rotten tooth and landed on the ground with a resounding thud.

Silas wiped his brow and exhaled. "That should keep the Fae from escaping their world. But just to be safe I'd break up the stones when you have the time. It can be quite useful in construction."

"Thank you for your help, Master Silas," Adeline said, cradling Sylvie on her hip. "I don't know how we can repay you. We're not a rich village…"

"Please, don't trouble yourself," Silas said. "Bundersnoot

would eat you out of house and home given the opportunity."

"I heard that!" Bundersnoot didn't bother to look up from where he was napping on their wagon. Silas ignored him.

"You can repay me by keeping people away from this place. The world is dangerously thin here and you never know who else is…watching." Silas suppressed a shudder. "Anyway, we've got business back in Elade-voc to attend to. So many books, so little time. But if anything strange happens let me know."

"We will, Master Silas."

He climbed up into the wagon and took the reins, waving goodbye as they left. They were several miles from Twoforks when Bundersnoot finally woke up. "You know void iron doesn't come cheaply. Did you learn anything on the other side?"

"I'll have to do some digging when we get home, but it seems all the legends about void iron might be understating its power."

Bundersnoot was momentarily stunned when Silas recounted his harrowing escape. "No wonder the Empress made possess-ing it punishable by death."

"That's another thing I'm wondering about. Conventional wisdom says the barriers between our worlds are strong, writ into the fabric of the world itself. If Fae are to enter our world they have to be invited or summoned by someone already here."

"As I recall, yes. Why?"

"Well despite how much reading I've done over the years, I never heard of *anyone* summoning the Empress."

On Vampires

"I told you, I don't give a good goddamn who your mother is, I'm not casting any hexes!" Silas shouted as the little brass bell jingled. At that moment Silas was halfway up a ladder checking if he still had powdered fish feet so didn't immediately see who had entered the shop. With a grunt he started down the ladder. "I am a wizard, master of the Eight Schools, and far too old to be involved in childish squabbling. Granddaughter, what a surprise!"

She was just past the cusp of legal adulthood, tall and radiating good health that only the regular meals of a wealthy upbringing could provide. Her father would have to beat off suitors with a stick, poor man. She was dressed in a suit of fine traveling clothes: knee-high leather boots and riding britches, a white linen shirt covered by a blue damask doublet, woven with a floral pattern in gold. "Damnit, Silas, I'm not your granddaughter and I've got a problem."

"Well I can't call you Narses. I spent too long calling your grandmother that."

Narses laughed genially. "It *was* rather confusing as a small child having about six or seven people, some younger than my own parents, who all called you granddaughter. It was quite a shock when I found out most people only had four grandparents."

The elder Narses had been the leader of Silas's adventuring party and they had made extensive use of her estates as bases of operation over the years. In time the adventurers had become a collection of extended relatives to Narses's many children and grandchildren. She had been the heart and soul of that party and her death at a ripe old age left them rudderless. One by one the party members had drifted in their own directions and it had been years since Silas had last seen any of Narses's family.

"It's so very good to see you again," Silas reached out and clasped Narses's hand. "So what's the problem so big you decided you needed Uncle Silas's help?"

"I think I've got a vampire problem."

"You're kidding. They're vanishingly rare you know. Possibly extinct."

"Trust me, I didn't want to think it was a vampire either." Narses pushed her chestnut brown hair back from her face and leaned against the shop counter. "When they came to me I thought the villagers were overreacting. But I went out there and looked at the evidence myself; there's no doubt about it, it's a vampire."

"Is that baby Narses?" Bundersnoot emerged from the recesses of the shop and jumped onto the counter. "It is! I demand a tribute of food and exactly three belly rubs, no more no less. If you give me more than three belly rubs I shall bite you." Bundersnoot started headbutting Narses playfully and Narses laughed, scratching him behind the ears.

"Bundersnoot, by all the gods you *just* ate. Look at this!" Silas bent over and picked up a food bowl, thrusting it at Narses so she could see the cat's audacity. "There's still food in here!"

"I am bored with that food, it no longer pleases me. And yet I am still hungry."

"We'll see about the food later," Narses said. "I can make good on the belly rubs right now, though, so long as you don't scratch my hand."

"I make no promises, you may begin with the belly rubs." Bundersnoot flopped obligingly on the counter and Narses got to work.

* * *

"Why is it, in the Empress's holy name, that every time some sort undead menace crops up it is inevitably in some benighted swamp?" Silas gingerly dismounted from the wagon, vainly trying to find a dry patch of land. He winced as mud splattered over his boots and the hems of his robes. "Great. These will never be clean again."

"I think technically it's a bog." Narses had changed from her city finery and was dressed in practical homespun and mud-encrusted farm boots. She landed with a wet thud, ignoring the sucking mud and grime that splattered everywhere.

"Bogs, fens, swamps, marshes, they're all the same. Wet, dirty, and full of blood-sucking parasites both mundane and magical. Bundersnoot are you coming?"

Bundersnoot was pacing nervously back and forth on the seat of the wagon, looking at the ground dubiously. "You go on ahead, I'll stay here and guard the wagon. Lots of suspicious characters in these parts." Silas and Narses looked at the single street of the village which was currently empty of any residents. "Yep. Wouldn't want anybody stealing the magical equipment."

"Oh come on you big baby," Narses said. "It's just a little mud, you can wash yourself off later."

"Wash yourself with your tongue and you wouldn't say that," Bundersnoot objected. "Let me know when you find somewhere dry to stay." He climbed into a box of supplies and immediately dozed off. Silas and Narses shrugged and headed into the village. Someone had tried to improve the street by laying logs across to keep wagons from sinking into the mud but unfortunately, the logs themselves had been pulled into the all-consuming muck and only marginally improved the situation.

"So why in the name of the Empress do people even live here?" Silas asked.

"The land's too poor for them to do much farming so they're mostly peat miners. I really can't imagine how they eke out a living doing this but they've been here since grandmother Narses was a child. They pay the rents every year so I'm not complaining."

"Really that much money in peat mining?"

"Let's just say this isn't exactly the most profitable of my family's holdings." The duo walked past a collection of wattle-and-daub buildings to a large half-timbered building in the center of the village. A sign hung from the street-side wall, faded and badly peeling paint depicting the traditional mug of ale and loaf of bread. Silas and Narses tried to scrape the mud off their boots before entering the tavern but their efforts proved fruitless.

"Mistress Narses!" The landlady was a jovial woman in much the same manner of tavern keepers Silas had met the world over. "So good to see you again! And who's this?"

"Silas the Inestimable, a comrade of my grandmother's back in the day! He's come to help us with our problem."

"My lord!" The landlady curtsied with more enthusiasm than

grace. "A true honor to have a comrade of the old Lady Narses under our roof! Ask for anything you desire and I shall endeavor to make it so."

"Really, a dry room and some food would be enough. Oh, do you have a stable? We came with a horse and wagon but the road seemed a little rough."

"I'll have the stable boy go round and fetch it."

"Ask him to be careful of my cat. He's normally rather good-natured but the wet makes him most upset." Silas and Narses sat down at one of the long tables and the landlady brought over a couple mugs of the local ale. It was hearty and thick enough a spoon could stand upright in the mug and they took deep, appreciative sips. Silas bade the landlady to wait at their table for a moment. "I always believe in going to the source local gossip. Young Narses tells me that there's been a problem in the village."

"Aye, there certainly has been, it's been going on near six months now. At least that's when we think it started, but we're not certain. We buried Old Man Carnot around the new moon half a year ago. There's always a little mischief that time of month and that's how it started: rattling at the shutters, mysterious noises. We all wrote it off as youths having a bit of fun. But then the livestock started turning up dead. "

"You have to understand, we don't have a lot of livestock here in the village. In lean years they can be the difference between a hard year and starvation for us so we take care of the livestock as a village. To think any one of us would kill them is, well— I'd almost call it sacrilege. But it kept happening, month after month around the new moon. We found our livestock utterly savaged with huge chunks taken out of them."

"That could be wolves. Or bog ghouls. Or any number of

hungry things," Silas said.

"We thought that at first as well, but the thing of it was the bodies were utterly drained of blood." Silas and Narses shared a meaningful look as the landlady leaned in closer, speaking no louder than a whisper. "And I mean drained. With the way some of them animals had been chewed up you'd expect blood scattered like in a slaughterhouse. But there wasn't a drop of blood to be found."

"And then just three weeks ago Malraux turned up dead. We don't know what he was doing out in the bog at that time of night. He grew up here, same as the rest of us, and he knew better than to go walking in the bog at night. We thought maybe he'd fallen in and drowned so we turned out the entire village to search. But when we found him his body was just like the livestock: badly mangled and utterly drained of blood." When the landlady finished she looked very pale and very scared. "Master Silas, sir, will you help us?"

"I will certainly do everything I can," Silas said. "I'd like to examine Malraux's body, if there's no objection."

* * *

"Well, all the available evidence definitely suggests a vampire attack." Silas carefully drew the blanket over Malraux's body, covering the grisly remains. "The body is incredibly pale and there's none of the postmortem bruising from blood pooling in the extremities which indicates total exsanguination. There are very few creatures other than a vampire that will do that."

Silas turned and began washing his hands in a basin. "It doesn't look like any scavengers picked at the body, which is typical with vampire victims. Something about makes animals avoid their victims. But I've never known a true vampire to make such a mess of the job. A vampire is a precision predator, they'll take one, maybe two bites out of their victim. Malraux had his entire throat ripped out and it looks like someone tried to dismember him. There's trauma on all four of his limbs." Silas toweled his hands off and opened a thick notebook.

"Could it be another sort of predator? You said bog ghouls were a possibility."

"I don't think it's a bog ghoul. Ghouls hunt in groups and if they leave anything of their victims it's very clear the person was eaten. What happened to Malraux looks more like a mutilation and that excludes a whole mess of other predators. Predators generally don't kill something unless they mean to take a few good bites out of it."

"Maybe it was a territorial killing? I've known wyrms to kill other predators that enter their territory as a warning. It could have seen Malraux as a threat. Although that doesn't explain the loss of blood."

Silas paused on a page of the note book, frowning in deep thought. "Narses, have there ever been any battles nearby? It doesn't have to be a historic, important battle. A minor skirmish would count just as well."

"Well, there's the legend of Perdition Point," Narses answered, tapping her chin thoughtfully. "I don't know how true it is. They say back when the Empress walked the earth the local king had a mighty fortress surrounded by rich lands. When the Empress demanded his submission he sent her an insulting letter. Enraged by this petulance, the Empress decided to make an example of him and worked great magics, tearing his fortress apart and converting the land around it into a dismal swamp. The Empress then had the king executed in a particularly gruesome manner although it varies from telling to telling. All that's left are the ruins of the king's keep in the center of the bog."

"Hmm. If I had a penny for every story I heard about some local lord defying the Empress back in the day and paying a terrible price for their hubris I'd be a very rich man." Silas grumbled. "Are we able to visit those ruins?"

"Definitely, grandmother took me out there a couple of times when I was small. As long as you stay on the path there's nothing to worry about."

"I think we should pay these ruins a daylight visit."

* * *

"That's them, right over there. Grandmother said they were too recent to predate the Empress but not by much."

Silas had to admit, the ruins were appropriately thematic for a bog. The black stone foundations of what had once been a round tower crouched on a hillock, looming like a predator in ambush. Vines, moss, and other vegetation had grown over the tower, but a path along the crest of the hillock remained clear. "I don't like this," Bundersnoot whined from his perch on Silas's shoulder.

"Oh hush, you're perfectly safe from any water or mud as long as you don't move." Narses led the way, fighting the vegetation that was threatening to consume the path entirely.

"No, Narses, there is something seriously not right about this place. I can smell it in the air."

"That's probably the swamp gas you're smelling," Narses said, hacking at a particularly stubborn vine. "Perfectly normal."

"No, I can sense it too," Silas said. "There's a subtle wrongness to this place. Everyone stay on your guard." Silas could feel the hairs on his arm standing up despite the balmy atmosphere of the bog in the midday sun. Even in its dilapidated state the tower managed to exude an aura of menace. Something terrible happened here a long time ago and the land remembered. Blood could have strange effects on soil, he had seen that with his own two eyes.

Silas pushed past Narses and took the lead, marching up the narrow trail towards the ruins. The fronds brushed against his legs and everything was obscured by a fog rising from the water adding to the eerie sense of the place. They came to the entrance of the tower which was covered with a curtain of hanging moss, which Silas brushed aside and to look at the interior. In the distant past, this room had been an armory, based on the racks of tarnished bronze weapons, some still standing upright. There were blocks of stone scattered across the floor and the ubiquitous vegetation creeped throughout. "Yes, this is definitely the right spot. Now we've just got to…"

"Silas, look out!" The warning almost came too late. Silas ducked just as he heard the whistle of a blade go past his head. Bundersnoot yowled and jumped, landing on whoever had attacked Silas. There was a roar of pain as Bundersnoot dug in with his claws.

"Take this, you psychotic bastard!" Bundersnoot spat and there was another bellow of pain and a stream of blistering invective. With a final yowl Bundersnoot jumped off and fled into the rubble of the tower, quickly becoming invisible. However, he had bought Silas and Narses enough time to prepare.

"As I suspected," Silas said, brandishing his staff before him. There was a short, nasty looking man with an even nastier looking axe. His face was dominated by a huge, black beard as coarse as a bristle brush and he was dressed in enormous oversized boots and stout leather clothing. But his most noticeable feature was a massive stocking cap covered in blood. "A Redcap."

"This is my lair, wizard! It has been ever since the Empress smote the unbelievers here eight hundred years ago. What do you and your flea-ridden stray think you're doing here?"

"Fleas? Stray?" Bundersnoot was outraged but remained hidden in the rubble. "I'll have you know that I am a pure-bred temple cat and fleas wouldn't *dare* take a bite of me!" Everyone ignored Bundersnoot's protests.

"Folk in the village aren't exactly pleased with your behavior." Narses said. "We've come out to put an end to it."

The Redcap scoffed. "A dandy aristocrat, a has-been wizard, and a cat? You really think you have what it takes to defeat me? I've slain thousands of people and delighted in their slaughter." The Redcap approached with the graceful threat of a predator. He raised his bronze axe and its edge shone in the sunlight. "What possible plan could you have to defeat me?"

"This." In a fluid movement Silas swung his staff, thwacking the Redcap over the head and knocking off the eponymous headgear. Narses caught the hat in midair, exclaiming with triumph. The Redcap growled and swung his axe towards Narses, who barely managed to dodge the attack.

"Silas, what do we do now?" Narses continued to duck and weave as the Redcap attack.

"Bundersnoot, now!" Bundersnoot shot out from the rubble and jumped into the air, snatching the cap out of Narses's hands with his mouth. Landing behind Silas, Bundersnoot quickly disappeared through the open doorway and into the swamp.

"No!" The Redcap turned to chase Bundersnoot but Silas tripped him. He dropped the axe and pushed himself back up, staggering towards the door. He didn't get very far before Narses tackled the Redcap and forced him to the ground."My hat! I need my hat!" The Redcap groaned, clutching his head which had started turning to stone. "No! No, no, no, give me back my hat you bastards!" The scream he let loose was high and terrified. The patches of stone spread until they covered his mouth and stifled his voice. Then, the Redcap toppled over and they watched as the rest of his body petrified.

"Did you know that was going to happen?" Narses asked.

"Well, I didn't know *that* would happen," Silas answered.

"So glad I brought you out here, Silas. Truly a brilliant mind."

"Silas, Narses, are you both okay?" Bundersnoot walked back into the tower, without the blood-soaked cap.

"Not even scratched, Bundersnoot," Narses said.

"Safe and sound. This plan went much better than I expected." Silas pointedly ignored the look from Narses. "Where did you put his hat?"

"It's a few yards back up the trail under a bush."

"Good. We'll want to destroy *this*," Silas kicked the hunched over statue on the posterior, "as soon as possible." Silas looked through the racks of weapons and found a solid bronze mace. Silas swung the mace down and the stone cracked, one of the Redcap's arms severed. "Once we're done breaking him into pieces we can dump them into the bog. I'd like to see him come back from *this*, the murderous bastard."

* * *

There was a palpable atmosphere of relief in the village when news spread that the Redcap had been defeated. The peat-miners weren't the sort of people to celebrate excessively, life on the edge of the bog was too hardscrabble for that, but an extra round of ales were downed in the tavern that night. Silas did not breathe easy until he had safely sealed the Redcap's dried cap in a glass container etched with magical runes, which he placed at the bottom of a crate of mundane supplies and covered it with root vegetables. If even one drop of human blood should fall on the cap it was possible the Redcap they had so laborious turned to gravel could return. Once they were in Elade-voc Silas intended to destroy the cap in his safest laboratory.

"That *should* be the end of the killings in the village" Silas said, dropping onto a bench across from Narses. "I would recommend everyone still stay away from the ruins. I *think* we managed to clear out any magic but with ruins that old you can never be sure."

Narses tapped her mug against his and took a well-deserved sip of ale."I appreciate you coming out here to handle this, Silas. Knowing what we know now, I feel kind of silly telling you it was a vampire."

"I thought it was a vampire as well, but the mangling of the bodies didn't make sense. All of the vampire species are very selective in their killings, very clean. By contrast, Redcaps are absolutely *brutal* with their victims. They have, —I don't know, I'd almost call it a need to torture their victims and prolong their suffering. Once a Redcap's finished with someone you usually have to put what's left in a bucket."

"Well what about Malraux, though? Because what happened to him…"

"Doesn't fit either pattern. I just feel like I'm missing *something.*"

"There's been another murder!" A band of villagers broke into the tavern carrying a burden between them. "Seigre's dead!" The villagers dragged the body of the poor Seigre into the tavern and deposited it on one of the common room's tables. Narses, Silas, and even Bundersnoot came over to investigate. Seigre's body was pale, even for a corpse, and his skin was wrinkled like dried fruit. On his neck were the two unmistakable bite marks of a vampire.

"I can smell grave dirt," Bundersnoot said. "We've got us a vampire, all right."

"What happened?" Silas asked. "Was anybody with him when it happened?"

"I was walking back with Seigre from the peat mines." A man of middle age stepped forward, still carrying his wooden spade. "We had just come back into the village and some…thing came down from a roof. Before I could react it jumped back onto the roof with Seirge. I raised the alarm and we started searching the village. That's when we found—what was left of him."

"We need to get everyone somewhere safe," Silas said. "Do you have a building made of stone? Somewhere strong and fortified?"

"There's the temple," Narses said. "I think it's the only stone structure in town. My grandmother paid for its construction."

"Good, pious woman, your grandmother. Narses, I need you to get everyone in the temple, bolt the doors and take shelter. Don't come out until Bundersnoot and I say it's safe."

"But you need my help!" Narses protested.

"Narses, listen to me." Silas took her by the shoulders firmly. Her face was the same as the six-year-old girl he remembered who wanted so desperately to fight trolls with her grand-mère. "The Redcap was one thing, that was a danger I was confident we could handle in broad daylight. There are no less than twenty-three different species of vampires and I have tools that can handle most of them. But there is a one in five chance that I cannot kill this creature. If it doesn't work, I need you to get everyone out of this village come sunup. No delay, no waiting, they take everything they need to survive and go. You find the Guilds and you get them to help you. Do you understand?"

"But I…"

"Do you understand, Narses?"

"Yes…Yes,—all right."

"Good woman, now go!" Narses and the villagers headed out of the tavern, carrying as many torches and lanterns as could be found and headed into the temple. Silas didn't rest easy until he heard the solid wood doors of the temple thud shut and the bolt slam home.

"Is consecrated ground really going to help them?" Bunder-snoot asked.

"Sacred ground sometimes helps but the main thing is it's solidly constructed and everyone's in one place. The last thing we need is the vampire picking them off one by one. They stand a better chance of defending themselves together than separately." Silas had seen it happen before, some fifty years back before he met Narses with an adventuring party he barely remembered.

Their party had been asked to clear a chateau for a wealthy patron and they needed some fast money. Clearing the entire building would have taken ages if they'd done it as a group so they decided to split up to cover as much ground as possible and regroup for any serious threats. None of them suspected the noblewoman was in truth a vjesci, feeding off the adventurers she could lure into the chateau. One by one they had been picked off until only Silas and Patricio, a knight armored in bronze and faith, remained. They had fled from that chateau as it burned in the night, never sure if they had been followed.

Silas emptied his pack on a table and sorted through the various tools and supplies he'd brought with them. He selected a handful of components and placed them in his belt pouch. He finally selected a wooden stake carved from a solid branch of ashwood. "All right, Bundersnoot, let's hunt us a vampire."

Silas and Bundersnoot stepped into the deserted village street. The only light came from the stained-glass windows of the solid, reassuring bulk of the village temple at the far end of the street. The rest of the village was shrouded in darkness and Silas looked up at the still-new moon. "Bundersnoot, can you sense them?"

Bundersnoot blinked and took a deep sniff of the air. "Down there," he nodded towards the eastern edge of the village. "Grave dirt and fresh blood. Definitely a vampire."

"All right, stay close." Silas muttered a spell and brought a flame of green wytchfyre into being, cradled in his hand. It provided some flickering illumination but it was little help in the oppressive darkness. Silas and Bundersnoot walked slowly, striving to not make any sound on the creaky walkways of the village. They reached a gap between two buildings and Bundersnoot paused, ears perked. He flicked his tail and pointed it towards the narrow space.

Without further warning Silas jumped and flung the ball of wytchfyre into the alleyway where it flared and burst as it hit the ground. The flash of green light lasted for only a second but it was enough to make the vampire scream in surprise. The vampire was about as tall as a full-grown adult but consisted of little more than a skeleton wrapped within a bundle of skin.

Instead of arms the vampire had two large, membranous wings and a swollen, distended stomach that Silas could only assume was engorged with stolen blood.

There were five vampire species that had wings in their humanoid form, all of them closely related and incredibly deadly. But fortunately for Silas all of those species were particularly susceptible to the power of the divine. Silas reached into his belt pouch and closed his hand around a vial of sanctified oil. He splashed its contents on the vampire, making it shriek in pain.

Silas attempted to draw the ashwood stake but the vampire recovered quickly and jumped on him. Malformed hands at the ends of its wings grabbed Silas's wrists, keeping him from utilizing any of his tools. Its strength was all out of proportion for its skeletal frame and it managed to pin Silas to the ground. The vampire hissed again and opened its mouth, filled with needle-sharp fangs. Silas kicked and bucked, but the creature remained clamped to his body.

Adrenaline surged through Silas's body and he desperately wriggled to get free, utilizing muscles he didn't realize he even had. He was fueled by a primal need to get free of this creature. Silas wanted to stand up, take a rock, and bash the vampire's head over and over until it was nothing but shattered bone and splattered brains. He was a wizard, for gods' sake, this wasn't how he was supposed to die! But even with all that, he could not escape. The vampire was about to sink its fangs into his neck when Bundersnoot landed on the vampire's wings with his claws extended.

It does not matter who or what you are, when ten pounds of very angry cat lands on an unarmored and extremely sensitive part of your anatomy, you're bound to take notice. The vampire shrieked again, Silas completely forgotten, as it flailed desperately to get Bundersnoot off its back. Bundersnoot dug his claws in deeper, ripping ghastly tears through the thin wings as the vampire tried to shake him off. Desperately, it attempted to fly away to escape its tormentor but the damage to its wing was too great. The vampire crashed back to the ground with even more agonized shrieks,

Silas drew the ashwood stake and kicked the vampire onto its back just as Bundersnoot leapt away. Aiming the stake, he drove it up under the ribcage towards where the vampire's heart should be. Ink black ichor gushed out, spilling onto Silas's arm and he withdrew in disgust. The vampire rattled and gasped, feebly attempting to pull the stake from its chest, but it was too slick for the creature to gain purchase. It gave a last wheezing croak and collapsed as the last of the blood poured from its mortal wound.

Bundersnoot circled the vampire, warily, checking for any movement. Satisfied that their foe had been defeated he turned to Silas. "Silas, are you injured? Did that thing manage to bite you?" Silas took a look over his body. Nothing *felt* broken, and Silas had broken quite a few bones in his adventuring days, but the light was so poor Silas couldn't discern much beyond that.

"It didn't get a chance to bite me, thanks to your efforts. We should incinerate this," Silas tapped the vampire's corpse with his boot, "as soon as possible. Can you sense anything else lurking about in the dark?"

Bundersnoot closed his eyes and concentrated. "I smell some traces but that could be his trail. I'll take a quick look around." Bundersnoot turned around and disappeared in the darkness. Silas bent over and pulled the stake out of the vampire's chest. It made an awful sucking sound as it came free. Silas had once seen a man take a chest wound thirty years ago and it had sounded a lot like that; the man had lasted longer than the vampire, but not by much.

Silas grabbed the vampire under the armpits and heaved. It wasn't terribly heavy but the fight had taken a lot out of him. "And I used to think Narses saying she was too old for this sort of thing was a joke." With a grunt he dragged the vampire to the edge of the village. After a little searching Silas managed to find a stack of dried peat that had been harvested some time ago. Silas hoisted the vampire on top of the stack of peat and with his remaining energy summoned another ball of wytchfyre to light the fuel. Soon the peat was burning steadily and a thick oily smoke was rising from the vampire's corpse.

"I checked its backtrail," Bundersnoot announced, walking up and rubbing against Silas's legs. "That was the only one so I think we're safe."

"Catch a whiff of anything else? I hate to think there's a third creature out there just waiting to jump on us when we think we're safe."

"If there is a third creature they're not out tonight so I'm going to bed." Bundersnoot paused and looked at Silas. "Are you coming?"

"No,—not just yet. I want to see this through to the finish."

"All right, don't stay up too late." Bundersnoot gave Silas's leg a headbutt and then he walked back into the village.

* * *

"If anything happens during the next full moon, send a message to us in Elade-voc. Empress willing you won't have any more trouble." Silas jumped up into the wagon and picked up the reins. Bundersnoot was already snoozing on a crate, enjoying the morning sun.

"We won't forget your work here, Master Silas," the landlady curtsied. "I have no idea how we could possibly repay you."

Silas heard Narses stifle a chuckle, but when he turned to the woman next to him Narses looked as sober as a judge. Silas turned back to the landlady. "Please, I couldn't in good conscience take something you might need in the future. Remember, if anything happens send word to Elade-voc" Silas clicked his tongue and with a wet squelching sound the horse pulled the wagon out of the mud.

"Does this mean I don't have to pay you either?" Narses asked.

"Hell no, you're getting a detailed invoice when I get back to my shop. You're rich enough to afford my prices and you made the mistake of dragging me into this mess."

"And it's a good thing I did, too. Empress beyond, a vampire *and* a redcap working together. If I'd ignored this and chalked it up to peasant superstition, who knows how many they would have killed?"

"In the short term? One or two a month, perhaps less than that. In the long term? A great many. Vampires and redcaps, they're parasites, they'll attach themselves to a community and feed off of people for decades. Centuries if they can manage it." Silas spat over the side of the wagon. "Best to burn out such diseases when they're discovered."

Silas winced as he thought about the scrape bound up beneath his sleeve. In the morning sunlight it had looked clean enough, and the vampire's mouth hadn't come anywhere close to it. But there had been so much blood when he thrust the stake in. Could some of its blood have contaminated the wound? Then again, every wizard worth their salt knew those stories of vampiric contagion were a bunch of superstitious nonsense and misinformation. Everyone knew that.

Didn't they?

59

On Parsley

"But I'm hungry!" Bundersnoot whined.

Silas was about to argue but then he heard his own stomach gurgle. "What time is it anyway? Noon?"

"Mealtime!" Bundersnoot announced confidently.

"There should be a village around here, they're scattered all across the Ganorne River valley, some of the best farmland in the known world." They'd been walking since early morning following a lead on a potentially interesting grimoire with answers to nagging questions Silas had about his encounter with the vampire. Silas winced again and rubbed his left arm where the wound remained unhealed. A crusted scab kept it from weeping blood, but the skin around the wound remained red and inflamed.

Unfortunately when they arrived the book turned out to be an ancient farming manual. Silas paid far too much for it, but he was sure he could find a book dealer in Elade-voc that would be interested. If they could get back to Elade-voc.

"Silas did you get us lost again?"

"We're on a road aren't we?"

"So?"

"Roads go *somewhere*, that's why they're roads."

"Turn back!" Silas almost stumbled over his own feet when

someone shouted at him. He turned to find a wizened old man rattling a rowan wood staff. Tied to the staff was a massive collection of holy symbols associated with a pantheon's worth of deities. "I warn you stranger, turn back on the road you're on! The village of Mauvaisane is cursed I tell you, cursed! We must make obeisance to the gods and pray for their mercy!"

"Oh thank goodness, there *is* a village!" Silas said. "Where is this village, elder?"

"Just a mile down the road that way!" The man pointed in the direction Silas and Bundersnoot had been going.

"Thank you kindly, elder. May the Empress go with you." Silas started walking towards the village but the old man shoved his staff in Silas's face.

"Take heed, stranger! Take heed! There are fell deeds happening in Mauvaisane! Turn back!"

Silas gently pushed the old man's staff out of the way. "Thank you, elder. Your concern is greatly appreciated but I think we'll be fine."

"You don't understand!"

Silas sighed in frustration. "I don't have time for this." Silas muttered a cantrip and summoned a ball of wytchfyre into his palm. "Listen to me, old man! I am a wizard, do you understand? A full-fledged wizard, not some mere vagabond conjurer! I have faced down demons, dragons, and gods alone know what else and lived to tell the tale. So unless you have something more than vague omens of doom, something specific that I *should* be concerned about, I shall bid you good day. Do I make myself clear?"

The old man nodded nervously as Silas dispelled his wytch-fyre but would not let Silas leave without one last warning. "There's something wrong with the people in the village. The young people, they've become inflamed with lust and have begun having bacchanals in the street! Nothing can stop them, and they tear anybody who tries to stop them apart with their bare hands. My daughters were taken up a week ago, I tried everything but they wouldn't listen to reason."

Silas paused and thought. "That *is* concerning. Thank you for your warning, elder. We'll be on our way."

"The gods go with you, master wizard. May they aid you where they failed me."

Silas handed the old man a silver coin for his trouble and rearranged his satchel. Once they had walked a good distance down the road, leaving the old man behind, Bundersnoot suddenly asked a question."Silas, what's a bacchanal?"

"Human mating ritual, you wouldn't be interested."Silas answered flatly, his mind clearly on other matters.

Bundersnoot tsked with annoyance. "Honestly, if you humans had the good sense to just mate wherever was convenient like cats, instead of complicating the matter so much. And your rituals, *spare* me your rituals. You can't just come out and *say* you wish to mate with someone. No, you have to do this elaborate dance. I like her, does she like me? On and on it goes."

"You think I understand it either? Utter insanity. Imbalance of the humors is what it is, an excess of the sanguinary spirit. Every person under—sixty, no sixty-five—ought to be leeched come springtime. Every single one of them."

"So this is a normal occurrence?"

Silas stopped and sighed, running his hands through his hair. "Maybe? Possibly? It's hard to say without further context. You know how humans are…messy and complicated?"

"I am extremely familiar, yes."

"In all my years and all my travels I have found humans are

consistent in their inconsistency. What the old man told us *may* be accurate. There may be young people coupling in the streets, violently attacking anyone who tries to stop them. I have seen stranger things in my time. It may just be he was the town's most pious man and the young people having fun made him finally snap. Until we know more I refuse to pass judgment."

"But we're going to walk in prepared?"

"Of course, I've managed to survive this long. I'd be terminally foolish to not heed any warning."

Within a quarter hour, they finally arrived at Mauvaisane which appeared like a perfectly normal farming village. Fields of barley were ripening in the sun and the sounds of barnyard animals could be heard. Mauvaisane had grown around a crossroads where two main roads intersected. Almost all the buildings faced directly onto the main roads with the village tavern, temple, and the bronzesmith occupying places of prominence at the crossroads. Everywhere people were going about their regular business.

"I'm not sure how I feel about this," Silas said. "Everything feels too *normal*."

"It smells fine to me," Bundersnoot said. "Although…" Here he cocked his head, trying to listen to something far away. "No, never mind, probably not important anyway. I don't know why you're so worried."

"I must be getting paranoid in my old age. Something about that old man spooked me, I guess."

"You haven't been partaking of the Devil's Oatmeal have you, stranger?"

Silas nearly jumped six feet in the air and squawked with surprise. Somehow an elderly woman, a respectable matron of the village if appearances were to be believed, was standing there appraising Silas as if he was something her cat had brought her. He tapped on his chest a few times just to make sure his heart was still inside. "Your pardon, good mistress. You took me by surprise."

"Not many travelers through here recently. Strange to see one such as yourself. And a cat. Gives a woman reason to believe you might be…" she gave him an appraising look, "…up to something. I ask again, stranger, you been partaking of the Devil's Oatmeal?"

"I'm sorry, I have absolutely no idea what on earth you're talking about," Silas said.

"The Herb of Death! Ache! Parsley, you damn fool!"

"Parsley?" Silas asked in confusion.

"Aye, you never seen parsley? Too high and mighty to do the cooking yeself, are ye? Bet ye never even set foot in an herb garden!"

"No, I'm familiar with parsley," Silas said, trying to gain some semblance of control over this conversation. "I've just never heard it referred to as Devil's Oatmeal before."

"Mark my words, young man, it be what's driving the young folk mad with lust and no mistake."

"Parsley," Silas responded flatly. "Small, green, leafy herb. Usually used as a seasoning with meat dishes? Sometimes served as a garnish? We are talking about the same plant, yes?"

"Yes, parsley! Although I be telling everyone in the village to pull theirs up. Something wrong with the soil this year."

"I assure you, madam, the extent of my interest in your village extends to a meal and directions to Elade-voc. Those taken care of we will gladly be on our way."

"Sees that you do, stranger." And with no further comment she returned into her home and slammed the door behind her.

"Well that was odd," Bundersnoot said with heavy understatement.

"As far as strange days go, this doesn't even crack the top fifty," Silas said. "Then again, the day's only half over so there's plenty of time left."

"And yet, I remain unfed."

"All right, let's get you some lunch."

* * *

When he had been a mere student, knowing only a handful of cantrips and just the basic elements of magic, Silas had developed the bad habit of reading while he ate. Some people would argue that reading during meals was a bad habit because it precluded the option for conversation. Silas's teacher had told him it was a bad habit because he kept getting gravy stains all over her magic texts which were *quite* irreplaceable *thank you very much* and he had no business reading material so above his level anyhow.

Now that he was himself a grumpy old wizard with his own books, Silas at least understood the desire to keep food from soiling them. But field notebooks, written in his own private cipher, were perfectly acceptable. "Why have I never sat down and done any research on parsley?" Silas asked, mostly rhetorically, as he went back and forth through his botany notes.

Bundersnoot looked up from his plate of cooked fish. "Did you have any reason before today to believe that parsley had any magical properties beyond making soups and roast meats taste better?"

"No, but that's not a reason to overlook it! What about all my research into dandelions? Who knew that a bowl of dandelion syrup would work just as well as a medium for scrying as purified water?”

“Probably nobody because first of all getting a large quantity of purified water is easier than getting an equivalent quantity of dandelion syrup. But secondly, and more importantly, you only started down that chain of research because the only things that grew in your windowbox were dandelions since you never watered it!”

Silas waved these points aside with his hand. “Still, if there’s so much folklore surrounding parsley, why hasn’t it been written down?”

“By all the gods, take me now!” Silas and Bundersnoot looked up at the sudden shouted statement to find a young couple engaged in…well, if it wasn’t public indecency yet, it was certainly headed in that direction. The handful of people in the tavern quickly ran out, fearing contagion from the madness of the two youths. Silas sighed and stood up.

“I suppose lunch shall have to wait.” Silas poked around the kitchen of the tavern until he managed to find a reasonably clean bucket. After filling the bucket with water from the well, Silas returned to find Bundersnoot observing the couple with clinical interest.

“Silas, is this a bacchanal?”

“No, I think there needs to be more people for it to be a bacchanal. This is just screwing.” Silas poured the cold water over the couple and shouted. “Hey! You two cut that out! It’s indecent for you to…oh. Oh gods. All right, that did not work.” The couple had not yet moved out of their clothing but the addition of cold water had inspired them to start. “All right, we’re leaving now.”

“But it had just gotten interesting!” Bundersnoot protested

as Silas picked him up off the table.

"Human. Mating. Ritual." Silas said through gritted teeth as he left the tavern.

"So, you see what I been talking about, have you?" The old woman from earlier was standing outside the tavern with her arms crossed. "Will you be taking my warnings about the Devil's Oatmeal seriously now?"

"It wasn't the parsley, though," Bundersnoot said. "I couldn't smell any of it on them. Besides which, they had been ensorcelled. I could see it as clear as day."

Both the old woman and Silas looked at Bundersnoot in disbelief. "What do you mean they were ensorcelled?" Silas asked. "You let me waste time fetching water when there were magics about?"

"You didn't tell me what you were doing! You get so bent out of shape over this sort of thing…"

"Is that cat really talking?" the old woman asked, interrupting their argument.

"Honored elder, this is Bundersnoot. He is a mostly normal cat with some magical enhancements due to the nature of being my familiar. My name is Silas, a wizard of extremely minor renown from the city of Elade-voc."

"Feed me!" Bundersnoot exclaimed.

"Pay him no attention, he already ate. What do you mean ensorcelled?"

"I would say it's very close to the sort of influence a…" Bundersnoot lowered his voice, as if trying to avoid attention, "a member of the Fae—can do. Very similar but not precisely the same."

"Now *that* I don't like. Damn, I hate being caught like this. We haven't got tools, we haven't got books."

"A wizard doesn't know what to do? Empress have mercy on all of us. Suppose I should just go lie down in the graveyard now." The old woman threw her hands up in the air in frustration. "Don't know why I bother warning anybody."

"Elder,—I'm sorry, I never learned your name."

"Celine."

"Elder Celine, we need to go somewhere safe. May we use your house?"

"I suppose so. Follow me."

Mauvaisane was not a large village so it took very little time for them to arrive at Celine's house. Silas finally put Bundersnoot down on a table and dumped out his satchel. "All right, I've got one field notebook, a pencil, replacement leads, a pouch of coins, my stick, spare socks, aaaaaand that's it."

"You brought spare socks but you didn't bring magical components? This is the last time you're packing unsupervised."

"It was five miles from home! I was expecting the possibility of wet socks, I didn't expect to run into trouble! All right, let's think. We have people being stirred into lustful frenzy, and the involvement of some entity that is probably capable of manipulating emotions."

"Such as that out there?" Celine pointed through the shutter and Silas joined her. The man that was strolling along the street was tall and extremely handsome. At least, Silas guessed he was handsome, he was never a very good judge of this sort of thing. He walked into Mauvaisane with an easy confidence, as if he had always belonged in the village and was just coming back from some trifling errand. He was dressed in a cream-colored linen shirt, which was unlaced enough to display his pectoral muscles in the sunlight. His breeches were black velvet, clearly of exquisite quality but in an understated way, and his knee-high boots were immaculate with none of the dust of the road.

As the man approached everyone from adolescence to well into middle age were overcome by their physical urges. They paired off and began engaging in extremely heavy physical affection ignoring everything else happening around them but especially the well-dressed stranger. He smiled as he watched the villagers indulge in physical delights and Silas could see a sort of shimmer around the man as magical energy was transferred.

"That," Silas said, "Is exactly what we're looking for. Come on, Bundersnoot." Silas picked up his staff and walked into the street, trying to project a confidence he really didn't have. Bundersnoot stepped into the street behind him and a tortoiseshell cat immediately approached and started rubbing against him.

"Well hello there," Bundersnoot purred. "What's a fine-looking kitten like yourself doing in a place like this?"

"Bundersnoot! Focus!"

Bundersnoot shook his head and stepped away from the affectionate tortie. "Right, sorry. On it. Ooooooh, that feels so nice." Bundersnoot arched as the tortie continued to rub against him. "How about you and I ditch these humans and get to know one another?"

"Bundersnoot! I swear by all the gods!"

"Sorry, chief, got some business to attend to."

"Bundersnoot, you are the absolute *worst* familiar." Bundersnoot sauntered off without a care in the world, leaving Silas to face the handsome stranger. Before Silas could address the man a woman approached him seductively. Her hair had come loose from her braids and she spread it out with her hands which in turn made her shift droop to expose a generous amount of cleavage.

"Is it true what they say about a wizard's staff?" she asked, and then she bit her lip as she reached to toy with Silas's staff. Silas jerked back from her in irritation.

"No. I've heard all the jokes and I've found none of them funny. Stand aside, I have work to do."

"Surely it can wait for later. There are so many other things I'd like to do with you."

"And yet there is *nothing* in the world right now I am interested in doing with you. Good day, ma'am." Silas strode past the woman without even a look back and the stranger narrowed his eyes in suspicion at Silas. The stranger shrugged and with a gesture a handsome young man came towards Silas instead.

"Hey there, want to make some magic together?" he asked, stripping his shirt off and exposing his muscles well-honed from years of farm work. "I'm sure you could put me under your spell."

Silas groaned in frustration and addressed the stranger. "Really? This is the best you can do?"

"Oh I assure you, I can do *so* much better," the young man said as he reached for Silas's staff. Silas pulled back again, careful to keep the staff out of reach of the villager. Suddenly a half-remembered piece of information jumped into Silas's brain.

"This is your *only* trick, isn't it? You're a succu-, no it'd be incubus with you, wouldn't it?"

"Concubus, technically." The stranger finally deigned to speak. "I must admit, wizard, I am rather impressed with your fortitude. I have seen people far more pious than you fall sway to my temptations much more easily. But perhaps there is something else I can offer you."

"You can offer to leave the people of this village the hell alone, leave, and never come back is what you can offer. And I won't hurt you if you do it willingly. Not too much, anyway."

The concubus laughed. "There is no harm done here. I have merely allowed the people of this village to express emotions they would have otherwise kept hidden. Such sexual yearnings, bottled up like fine wine. It makes a delicious vintage when it's finally released. And indulging in the pleasures of the flesh is perfectly natural."

"So is arsenic," Silas replied bluntly. "Spare me your trite rationales, I have no patience for them. Your emotional manipulation isn't natural and you're a parasite, feeding off of the lifeblood of others because you cannot produce it yourself. Now get the hell out of my sight before…"

"What if I were to give you the knowledge you seek?" Silas reached towards his wound by reflex and the concubus smiled. "Yes, I can see the emotions clouding your mind quite clearly. You are plagued by fear and need reassurance. I could give you that, not for free of course. But we could make an exchange. Just let me drink my fill of this village and go on my way and I shall give you the answer you seek. A reasonable price, is it not? There will be no permanent harm to the villagers, and you will no longer be plagued by uncertainty."

There was a long moment while Silas paused and thought. He was tempted, oh so sorely tempted, he could make no denial of that fact. He had hoped the grimoire would answer the question that kept him awake at night. Was this wound something to worry about? Was he going to wake one day to find himself turned? Was there anything he could do to prevent it? Silas prided himself on his knowledge, his ability to discover tiny details of esoterica which gave him an edge in countless battles. But you couldn't know everything and Silas was troubled by his ignorance.

And what would be the harm? A small baby boom nine months later? Hardly a catastrophe. Some people might welcome such an occurrence. Yes, they might find their spiritual energies a little depleted, but if the concubus moved on there would be no long-term harm. If.

Silas sighed. It was a real burden doing the right thing all the time. "No, I cannot make such a bargain. Using people as a means to an end is antithetical to me. Leave now, stranger."

"Or you'll do what?" the concubus sneered.

Silas stepped close to the concubus and lifted his staff in both hands. He paused only briefly before swinging the staff with all his might directly into the concubus's torso. The air whooshed out of the concubus and he folded over in half as Silas continued to beat him, refusing to relent, until the concubus was begging for him to stop.

"Please," the concubus moaned, all arrogance gone from his voice. "Please, I'll do whatever you ask. I'll make any promise you want."

"Release everyone in this village from your influence and leave them, never to return."

"I'll do it!"

"Swear by the name of the Empress that you will!"

"I swear! I swear in the name of the thrice-cursed Empress that I shall do all that you ask! Just stop hitting me with that stick!"

Satisfied with the concubus's promise, Silas finally stopped his assault. The concubus groaned in pain. "Release them. Leave and never return, parasite. Or by the Empress I shall vent the fury of a wizard upon you the likes of which you have never seen."

"It is done!" The concubus said, slowly climbing to his feet and groaning a little from the bruises. Even after getting the living daylights kicked out of him, the concubus managed to project a smoldering sexuality. "In all my years of wandering this earth I have never met a person capable of resisting my powers. What is your secret?"

"Clean living," Silas replied bluntly. When it became clear that the concubus would get no further answers, he sauntered out of the village in a way that managed to look effortless but most assuredly wasn't. Silas watched him leave, irritated that even after a thorough thrashing the concubus could exude such an aura of insouciance. "I should have set his hair on fire," Silas muttered.

Celine emerged from her home and took a look at the villagers slowly returning to their senses with varying degrees of embarrassment. "We're going to have a mess on our hands, and no mistake."

"Well, maybe in nine months there will be a few extra babies," Silas began.

"Oh yes, but I wasn't talking about that. I was talking about the fact that Lizbet's run off with Madeline's husband. And Lizbet's husband run off with Genevive's husband. And Genevive and Madeline have run off with each other. Who's going to sort that out, I ask you?"

"I suppose they could all run off with each other. I've seen it happen before. Back in my adventuring days I knew a polycule that was *infinitely* more complicated..." Celine gave Silas a look which would have given even the concubus pause and Silas's explanation trailed off.

"Well stranger, I suppose you've earned our thanks in spite of yourself—"

"Just a meal and directions back to Elade-voc would be more than sufficient," Silas said and Celine frowned at the interruption.

"Even if," Celine continued, "I could have handled it myself. If I'd known all it would take was a good thrashing I'd have cut a hickory switch and gone at it. But I'll make sure you get some bread and cheese before you leave." Celine pointed towards the crossroads. "Take the road leading east out of the village and you'll come to Elade-voc before nightfall. Now if you don't mind I've got a village to manage and parsley that needs re-bedding." She marched purposefully through the village, grabbing various people and shoving them towards work that needed doing while keeping up a stream of invective.

Silas waited at the crossroads, enjoying the midday sun as he snacked on the promised bread and cheese. About an hour later Bundersnoot finally reappeared, acting as if nothing untoward had happened at all and he had been napping this entire time. "There you are," Silas said and Bundersnoot looked at him guiltily. "Busy making our goodbyes are we? Or have we decided to move to Mauvaisane?"

Bundersnoot ignored this comment. "I don't suppose you remembered to get food for me this time?"

"No. And if you want supper we better head for home with no delay." Silas stood up, brushing crumbs from his robe, and started down the road to Elade-voc.

Bundersnoot growled with frustration and followed behind Silas. "Incidentally how did you manage to defeat that incubus?"

"Concubus technically. They didn't have anything to offer me."

"Not even the information you've been looking for?" Bundersnoot asked.

"If it was some other form of demon, possibly. But concubi and their ilk aren't the most intellectual of demons. At the end of the day all they can offer is sex. And who needs that nonsense?"

On Politics

It is a common misconception that the bite of a vampire can turn a mortal victim into one of the Accursed. The truth is far more complicated. Half-vampires and pseudo-vampires such as the vjesci, obayifo, and dhampyr are incapable of turning a mortal into the Accursed. Why they are incapable of spreading the curse when many of them were themselves turned remains a mystery. Some wizards speculate that it is because of their very mortal origins that these creatures lack the power to turn another.

Even the more powerful near-vampires, such as lamashtu or glaistig, cannot transform a mortal into one of their kind, despite their fiendish origins. It is only those creatures which I have classified as True Vampires that possess this power...

"All right," Silas thought, "but what is a *true* vampire? Why, why, why are you so dreadfully obtuse Mistress Toquer?" Toquer had been, and remained as far as much of the world was concerned, *the* expert on the countless variations of the undead known throughout Amastica. The downside was that she was so exceedingly exact in her descriptions that it became difficult to tell the differences.

Silas rolled his sleeve back and looked at the wound on his arm again. In the month since the incident in Mauvaisane the skin around the wound was no longer inflamed, but the scab had turned black and shiny. He picked up a ruler and measured it for the third time this day. The scab remained a hair under six inches long, but Silas was almost certain it had grown before he started measuring it. Guiltily he rolled his sleeve back down and would have continued reading but the shop bell rang and he was distracted from the incredibly thick book. His usual refrain died on his lips when he saw who had entered his shop.

"I'm told you're a man with knowledge of a great many things." The woman was flanked by two armed retainers in blue tabards bearing five gold circles, the livery of the Elade-voc city guard. She was tall and well-proportioned, obviously had never gone without a meal in her—thirty—no, must be closer to forty—years of life. She was dressed in cloth of silver and despite the early autumn heat she was wearing a collar of vair fur. Clearly a member of the uppermost ranks of the city's aristocracy and a member of the Council of Elders as well.

Silas emerged from behind his counter and bowed with great respect. "Your ladyship, I pray crave your pardon. I am but a humble scholar of the eight disciplines and always at the service of the Council of Elders. What brings you to my unworthy shop at this time of day?"

"You may recover, good sir. Tell me, what knowledge do you have of a being known as Yamlur'xex?"

Silas felt the blood drain from his body and the room seemed to get darker. "M'lady, you *must not* speak that name. Not even in the depth of your heart if you can help it. It will draw unwanted attention from forces best avoided." Silas pushed past the armed retainers and began pulling curtains over the shop windows, casting the room into a deep darkness only mitigated by the midday sunlight.

The noblewoman watched Silas's actions with some bemusement before continuing. "Master Silas, I fear time is very short so I shall be frank. Members of an organization calling themselves Revelers of the Obscene Feast are foretelling impending doom upon this city and the arrival of The Great Glutton Whom Consumes the World, Yamlur'xex…"

"DON'T! Say that name!" Silas trembled with fear utterly unrelated to the scowl on the woman's face and the presence of two heavily armed men. Silas took a deep breath and continued in a more even tone. "My lady, please, for all our sakes. Names have power, some more than others and that one more than most. Please believe me when I say that name must. Not. Be spoken."

"Well then what shall I refer to it as?"

"The Great Glutton, or perhaps just the Glutton. That,—that should be safe enough."

"Very well." The woman's faced returned to an expression of haughty command, a woman used to her words being obeyed and no questions asked. "As I said, I have intelligence that the Revelers seek to welcome the Great Glutton into our city. However, their communications are vague and unhelpful so I wish to know what they are threatening to do and what I should do to stop them."

"I see." Silas shuddered despite the warmth of the day and glanced at the guards. "My lady, pray do not take offense at this question, but how deeply do you trust your retainers?"

The two heavies glared at Silas but the woman gave them both an appraising look. "As much as I trust any other members of the city guard to do their job and protect the best interests of the city."

"Would you trust them absolutely and without hesitation?"

The woman paused, thinking before answering. "Not without

hesitation, no."

"I would request that you keep your guards outside the shop for this discussion," Silas said. "Even a little knowledge in this situation could be disastrous if applied incorrectly."

* * *

It had taken some convincing, but Lady Charlène Gavreau had finally given her grudging assent for her two armed retainers to wait outside Silas's shop. She was currently waiting in an inner chamber of the shop whose chief benefit was that it had no windows and thick stone walls. Silas often used it as a summoning chamber on the rare occasions he called upon beings from the other plane. Bundersnoot was watching as Silas dug through a pile of books trying to find a specific tome of arcane lore.

"Charlène was Lady Mayor before our current Mayor, Eugénie Larousse." Cats got everywhere in Elade-voc so Bundersnoot could always suss out local gossip if Silas ever needed it. "Scuttlebutt is that Charlène exhausted the Gavreau family's coffers to buy her election the first time and they haven't recovered since, hence the Larousse clan taking the chair. The merchant houses will be electing a new mayor in six weeks so the Larousses have been pretty open-handed recently."

"Anyone else a serious contender?"

"The Rouselles have been throwing money around but they don't have enough influence to pose a serious challenge to Eugénie. The Larousse have made things good for the merchants so it looks like she's got this sewn up tight."

"Where in the multiple hells did I put that madman's ramblings?" Silas grunted as he bent down and checked the bottom-most shelf. "I put it away somewhere I wouldn't lose it and now…"

"It's in the black desk, bottom-most drawer. You locked it with the scarab key. Anyway, so that suggests to me a very possible reason as to why Lady Gavreau is bringing this information to us now."

Silas dug through his pouch and found a ring of keys, fumbling until he managed to find the brass key engraved with a scarab sigil. "Of course, he came from Pewenet, that's why I used the scarab. Couldn't leave it lying around where anybody could see it." Silas kicked a sack of rags aside and unlocked the drawer. He gave a cry of satisfaction and took out a ragged papyrus scroll which he unrolled carefully to confirm its contents before returning it to its wooden case.

"Silas are you even listening to me?" Bundersnoot flicked his tail in irritation. "We're being used as pawns in a political game. If she defeats the Revelers and saves the city she could tip the entire election back in her favor. Or maybe the Revelers are just a bloody stupid drinking society and she's concocted this story to use you to eliminate her opponents! This is why we stay out of politics."

"She knew the name, Bundersnoot."

"What if she's a member of the Revelers herself and is making a play within the organization *as well as* the Council of Elders? The best cover for a conspiracy is another conspiracy."

Silas paused. "All right, you can sit in and watch her. If something feels off tell me, you're better at reading people than I am. Just…don't demand food."

"Well, if you fed me properly."

"Bundersnoot! By all the gods above and below, now is not the time."

"I know, now let's go see what this aristocrat wants."

Silas and Bundersnoot entered the summoning chamber and Silas carefully closed the heavy oak door behind him. The only light from the room came from a hooded oil lamp hanging from the ceiling which cast the room in flickering half-light. Lady Gavreau was sitting in one of two straight-backed chairs Silas had brought into the chamber on either side of a small table that normally held various magical components. Silas sat down across from Lady Gavreau and placed the scroll case on the table.

"Lady Gavreau, when did you first learn of the Revelers and the Glutton?" Silas asked.

"Approximately two months ago." Lady Gavreau looked straight at Silas, her expression hard and all business. "One of my operatives came across correspondence among members of the merchant houses that mentioned the Obscene Feast. About a week later my operatives reported that a party members of said merchant houses attended ended in a homicide. Naturally this was covered up as an incredibly tragic accident but…" Lady Gavreau smiled. "Blackmail has proven so useful in my career."

"I ordered my operatives to investigate further to see if this information could be used to my advantage. They discovered the names of important members of the Revelers, as well as numerous references to The Great Glutton Whom Consumes the World, Yaml-" Lady Gavreau stopped herself before Silas could interrupt. "Yes. Them. Within the last fortnight someone, I assume the Revelers, started killing my people. Of the operatives who remained, they found it increasingly difficult to obtain any information about what the Revelers are currently doing. I suspect the Revelers improved their operational security. And then I received this."

Lady Gavreau reached into her doublet and pulled out a scrap of paper. It was smeared with blood but the writing on it was mostly legible. "It was pinned to the body of one of my operatives who was dumped in front of my house in the early hours of the morning."

Silas took the note and carefully spread it out on the table. It was brief and to the point:

All is arranged, there is naught you can do to stop the coming of the Great Glutton Whom Consumes the World. Tonight Elade-voc shall fall in a final orgy of Revelry.

"Whatever they are doing it is happening tonight and I plan to stop it."

"She's telling the truth," Bundersnoot said. Lady Gavreau started when Bundersnoot spoke, surprised at a common house cat speaking. "I think she has ambitions about using this for her political career, but her motivations are at least partly genuine."

"Master Silas, these Revelers, whoever they are, have killed my people, threatened my home, and are endangering my city." Lady Gavreau's eyes were hard as flint and she frowned with determination. "I will pay any price to stop them."

"Very well. To begin, how much do you know about the nature of the universe?"

"I have never had reason to give it much consideration."

"A common metaphor is to say that our world and the Land of the Fae are like two sides of a tapestry: connected, made of the same fabric, and what happens on one side can influence the other. Often what seems like random and incomprehensible on one side appears as a glorious and intricate pattern on the other side. In the days of the Empress and the more powerful Empress-Regents travel between the two worlds was easier and rather common. Today it is still possible but far less frequent.

The important thing to remember, though is this: creatures from the Land of the Fae may be strange and terrible, but they at least have some fundamental similarities with us. Made of the same cloth, to further stretch an overburdened metaphor."

Silas opened the case and carefully unrolled the scroll. "This is a copy of a text originally written by a man from the distant land of Pewent. Writing this copy drove the scribe who made it mad."

"How can writing a scroll make a scribe take leave of her senses?"

"I suspect she was disturbed by the secrets revealed within this scroll. It deals primarily with beings referred to as Interlopers, although they've been called many things. The Old Ones, The Outsiders, The Elder Gods. They have as many epithets as there are languages in the world."

"But what *are* these Interlopers?"

"Their exact nature is unclear. Anyone who attempts to study them extensively finds themselves going mad or, well, draws their attention with fatal results. What little is agreed upon is this: The Interlopers come from outside our universe, of neither our world or the Fae and antithetical to both. Even at the peak of her power with the world at her feet, the Empress feared the Interlopers."

"So these Revelers, what are they attempting to accomplish?"

"In ancient times, some people venerated the Interlopers as gods, performing ruthless and inhuman rituals in an attempt to appease the Interlopers and steer their actions. I suspect that the Revelers are simply a new iteration of these ancient cults. What they hope to accomplish is irrelevant because any success in drawing the Glutton's attention to Elade-voc will result in the city's destruction. Why they think this is a good idea..."

Silas waved his hand in the air noncommittally. "Any number of reasons but none of them will be logical I'm sure."

"Will they really destroy the city? Our walls were laid by an Empress-Regent, bound by ancient magics. No siege has ever succeeded in taking the city."

"A city that withstands a siege can still be betrayed from within." Silas unrolled the scroll, found the relevant passage and began to read.

Four hundred years before the coming of the Empress the city of Noviomagus stood proudest and greatest among the wizardly city-states. Their rulers were powerful and cruel, striking fear into the hearts of their enemies. The people grew rich from the plunder of a hundred lands. But in their greatness the people of Noviomagus became proud and the mages of the city dared to command the sun, the moon, and the stars. So great was their hubris that they sought to command the Interlopers.

"We are wise and powerful," the wizards said. "Let us bend the Interlopers to our will, that we might spread our dominion across the earth and become unto gods." At the conjunction of the planets the wizards performed the Ritual of the Obscene Feast and summoned the Great Glutton. But no woman can control the Interlopers and the wizards were the first to fall to the Glutton's insatiable appetite. The entire city of Noviomagus, its women, its children, its cattle and chattels, all of it was consumed in the never-satiated maw of the Glutton. Even the walls of Noviomagus, built with great cunning and artifice, were torn down to feed the beast.

"Our enemies have fallen to their hubris," some of the wizards of lesser cities said. "Let us rejoice at their misfortune. No longer must we pay tribute and homage."

"They have fallen, yes," other wizard said, "But the Great Glutton remains unsatiated and shall consume us in time. We must act now

for our own preservation before it grows stronger."

Three hundred wizards, trained in the eight disciplines, formed a circle round the remains of Noviomagus. They called upon the bountiful earth and asked it to shake, opening a great fissure to swallow the fallen city. They called upon the mighty sea and asked it to send its tides, to flood down upon the city and cover it for all time. They called upon [illegible] to close the gate and bar the Interlopers unto the end of days. All this they did to save themselves from the Great Glutton Who Consumes the World and Noviomagus was forgotten. Thus fell the city of Noviomagus.

Silas looked up from the scroll. "A tad dramatic, perhaps, but accurate. If the Revelers are in truth active within the city we must stop them before they succeed in summoning the Glutton. Perhaps an Empress-Regent and a college of wizards could save us from the Glutton, but Tevioch is many, many leagues from here."

"Very well," Lady Gavreau said. "I shall have every spy in my employ locate where the Obscene Feast is being held this night. And then we shall strike."

* * *

"You're certain they're in that building?" Lady Gavreau asked. It was a mere hour from sunset and there was no margin for error if the Revelers were to be stopped. The building was an elegant townhouse situated in one of the higher-rent districts of Elade-voc. Most of the view of the townhouse was obscured by a six-foot high stone wall encircling the lot.

"I am, mistress," the spy said. She was a slight woman in a gray cloak that made her shapeless and uninteresting, easily ignored by even detailed observation. "I saw with mine own eyes twenty people on the list you gave us enter that house and I've had my urchins watching all the exits. Nobody has left."

"Excellent work. Have your urchins pull back, we're going to take it from here." Lady Gavreau had exchanged her merchant house finery for a gambeson, bronze breastplate, and stout canvas breeches. She was armed with a bronze sword and dagger, both of which she drew. "Jacques, take your men around the back of the building. Once you're in position send up a flare and break through the servant's entrance. We'll go through the front on your mark."

"Understood, m'lady." Jacques was a big slab of a man, over six foot and all of it muscle. "Capture or kill?"

"Capture so we can interrogate later but spare the servants. We're not after them and I don't want this turning into a bloodbath."

"By your leave." Jacques nodded and took half of the well-armed bruisers into the cramped alleys of Elade-voc. Silas was feeling terribly underprepared. He had donned some of his old adventuring gear and had a collection of magical components, but he didn't have any armor and the only weapon he had was his staff. Even a dagger would have made him feel better, but in the rush to prepare he had forgotten to bring one. Everyone else in the group was at least wearing armor and two or three weapons. There was the sound of metal scraping on metal as weapons were drawn and checked.

"Standard entry pattern. Gustav, you're on point." A big, blonde man from the far north, probably a member of one of the mercenary guilds, came forwards and nodded. He was wielding a huge, two-handed hammer that could crush anything smaller than a castle wall. Lady Gavreau turned to the wizard. "Silas and Bundersnoot, stay close to me and out of the action.

I don't want you getting hurt."

"Doesn't this remind you of your adventuring days?" Bundersnoot asked.

"Did a lot of damn stupid things in my adventuring days," Silas muttered. "Facing down a potential apocalypse? Most damn fool thing I've ever done." Silas thought back to the time he, Narses, and the others had decided to raid the hidden temple of some god-eaters on the mere rumor of finding histories written before the Empress. They had planned that mission for months and brought a full company of Narses's armed retainers as muscle and they still barely made it out alive. But Silas had thrilled in every minute of that adventure and even helped write a song about their deeds. He could only look to tonight with resignation and dread.

The sudden bang and flash of light from the flare almost made Silas jump out of his skin. He ran after Lady Gavreau and her squad, just in time to see Gustav smashing the wood gate into kindling without breaking stride. The entire squad ran through the ornamental garden, trampling the flower beds, and stacked up around the mahogany door. Gustav swung his hammer right where the lock was set into the door. There was a loud crack but the lock remained wedged into the doorjamb while the door swung away. Two men with axes charged into the house while a third with a crossbow covered them.

There was a cry of alarm from within the house and the crossbowman fired his weapon, the quarrel thunking into something obviously flesh. There were the sounds of a struggle and then one of the men shouted "Clear!" Lady Gavreau led the squad into the atrium of the house. This particular townhouse was constructed in the Imperial style, with a series of rooms built around a central courtyard that was open to the sky. A shallow pool formed the locus of the courtyard, surrounded by a number of ornamental plants. Otherwise the courtyard, and the house, appeared abandoned.

"Well, wizard, do you sense anything?" Lady Gavreau asked.

"Not yet, my lady," Silas stepped carefully over the splatters of blood across the mosaic floor of the atrium and joined her. "But a ritual of summoning need not take place in the open air."

With a hand gesture, Lady Gavreau directed her troops and they began searching the rooms connected to the courtyard. There was a crash of furniture being overturned as the soldiers investigated but no further cries of alarm or sounds of combat. "If this proves to be a wild goose chase, I shall be very upset with my spies," Lady Gavreau said.

There was a clatter of broken crockery and several servants ran screaming from the back of the house. They were followed by the squad of men led by Jacques who forced the servants to their knees in the courtyard. "We cleared the kitchen and the servants' quarters, m'lady," Jacques reported. "They appeared to be cleaning up."

"Who's in charge here?" One woman, approximately fifty, raised her hand. Lady Gavreau strode towards her and looked down with all the experience of someone born to command. "Is there anybody else in the house?"

"I don't know."

There was a loud smack and the housekeeper fell to the ground from Lady Gavreau's smack. "Lie to me again and I'll take it out on one of the scullery maids."

The housekeeper pushed herself up from the ground and spat towards Lady Gavreau. "I don't work for you, and you're not from the city watch so I don't have to tell you anything."

Lady Gavreau looked over the other servants, carefully

scanning her faces as most of them avoided her eyes. She stopped before one of the maids and bent down. The girl tried to avoid Gavreau's gaze but she grabbed the girl under the chin and looked into her eyes. "This one," she said. "Jacques, cut her head off."

"No!" the housekeeper screamed. Silas looked and although the light was bad he could see the family resemblance between the two women. "I don't know! I swear I don't know! They came to the house, thirty, maybe forty people. I didn't recognize all of them. We served them dinner and then they ordered us into the kitchen and told us not to come out. I don't know where they are, I swear."

"Nobody on the ground floor," Gustav reported, emerging from a room that looked thoroughly ransacked. "I have some men searching the upstairs now."

Lady Gavreau turned back to Silas. "Well, wizard. If you were holding a depraved arcane ritual, where would you be holding it?"

"Somewhere secure, not easily accessible to people I don't want interrupting," Silas replied. "Bundersnoot, do you sense anything?"

Bundersnoot jumped down from Silas's shoulder and took a deep sniff and turned his head about. "I smell incense, alcohol, and a lot of blood. I hear music, drums and horns but it's faint. Most importantly I can *feel* the magic underneath us, a deep throbbing." Silas paused to concentrate and he could sense the hum of magical energy as well. Bundersnoot paced back and forth, trying to get a fix on where the magic was coming from. "This way," Bundersnoot said as he trotted confidently towards the dining room of the villa.

The room was empty save for the three couches which imitated the Imperial style of banqueting. Bundersnoot inspected the room carefully, slinking under the couches and inspecting discarded dishes. Eventually Bundersnoot's ears perked up and he turned his head towards a fresco depicting the fertility goddess Etar with her human favorites. "There's music coming from behind there," Bundersnoot said.

"Gustav. Hammer." Gustav complied with Gavreau's order and the fresco shattered under the bronze head of his weapon. Behind the fresco was darkness and Gustav continued to swing his hammer, making the hole bigger, plaster piling at his feet. Silas summoned up some wytchfyre and sent it over Gustav's head, illuminating the secret room.

"A secret staircase," Silas groaned. "It's always a secret staircase. I *hate* insane cults."

"Gustav, make that hole big enough we can get through. Batu, round up everyone still searching the house and get them down here. Jacques, you designate five men to watch the servants, your most level-headed and reliable. If the servants start causing trouble they stop it by any means necessary, understand?" The men nodded to comply with their orders.

"My lady, if you will permit me a moment," Silas said and he gently nudged Gustav aside from the fresco. Silas stuck his head in the hole and by the illumination of wytchfyre took a look at the back side of the fresco. "As I expected," Silas said, and with some difficulty he managed to worm his arm through the hole as well. Silas grunted and the fresco swung out on concealed hinges. "Secret doors usually only need to be secret from one side. The mechanism is usually extremely obvious on the other."

Lady Gavreau looked around at her assembled retainers. "Standard hostile entry, assume anybody you find is a threat until confirmed otherwise. We will not be taking any risks, stopping the ritual is our paramount concern. Does everybody understand?" There was a chorus of assent and Jacques led his team down the stairs.

"More and more like old times," Silas said to Bundersnoot as they followed Lady Gavreau and her warriors down. "No guarantee we'll only run into cultists, of course. All manner of things could be down there. You remember that time with the slimes?"

"Please, don't remind me," Bundersnoot said. "Any time I think about that I can't bring myself to clean my fur for a week."

The base of the stairs proved that this was no dank and dingy catacomb, stumbled upon by accident and repurposed. It was clearly explicitly built with dry, well-dressed stone and garishly colored rugs covering the floor. The hallway was lit with wax candles that gave off far too warm and inviting light for the setting. About fifty feet down there was a bend in the hallway so whatever was happening wasn't immediately visible. The sound here was overpowering and it made speaking impossible. Lady Gavreau made motions and the squad spread to both sides of the passage. Silas didn't understand what they were communicating but he pulled a vial from his belt satchel. With a point of her hand the soldiers began a headlong rush down the hallway.

The room they entered was in many ways a duplicate of the dining room upstairs with three couches surrounding enormous table laden with a variety of foods and alcohols. Dozens of people were gorging themselves on food and drink, some vomiting from overindulgence. To one side a band consisting of a handful of horn players and two people enthusiastically beating on drums kept a frantic tempo pulsing in the room. All around the banqueters people were dancing and writhing in an erotic manner. Some had even progressed from dancing to equally enthusiastic acts of athleticism. At the far end of the room was a curtain dyed in the most exquisite purples concealing an inner sanctum.

The sheer wave of sound made communication impossible, so Lady Gavreau and her soldiers charged ahead. None of the cultists noticed as the warrior squad charged into the room. With a swing of his axe Jacques knocked down two horn players but the remaining band members continued to play, increasing the already furious tempo. Gustav, in a display of strength, upended the entire dining table and scattered dishes across the floor. The banqueters merely wormed their way off the couches and began eating food directly from the floor, oblivious to the doom descending upon them.Even when threatened at sword point the Revelers continued in their debauchery, the outside world having no effect on their hedonistic pleasures.

Silas wove his way through the chaos, pushing Revelers aside with his staff, marching towards the purple curtains. Nobody else seemed to notice the purple curtains, the obvious epicenter of this obscene ritual. Silas concentrated and he could sense tendrils of magic around the curtains, making them effectively invisible to all but a skilled practitioner. As Silas got closer he began to hear an arrhythmic chanting in a language not meant for human tongues. Silas felt physically ill just listening to this foul magic but he pressed onwards.

When Silas entered the inner sanctum, he was greeted by eight individuals standing in a circle, their naked bodies covered in painted runes. In the center of their circle was a white marble altar that was stained with old blood, and bound upon the altar was a terrified child. Just behind the altar was a portal similar to those Silas had encountered that led into the Land of the Fae. Similar enough to be familiar but different enough to be horrifying. The only thing Silas could make sense of seen through that portal was the starlit blackness of the night sky but most of the portal was covered with—thing—shaped like no living creature Silas had ever seen.

Abruptly, the chanting stopped. The person Silas presumed was their leader raised an obsidian dagger and prepared to plunge it into the heart of the sacrificial victim. Without hesitation Silas flung the vial in his hand with all his might towards the ritual circle. It broke and there was a loud bang as the quicksilver-infused gravel exploded. Silas gestured with his hand, spoke, and a blinding flash of colors joined the explosion. The cultists screamed in shock and broke the circle, some of them turning to meet this new threat.

"Seize him!" a voice ordered. "The planets are aligned! The ritual must be complete for me to enter your world! Seize the wizard and cut out his heart!" Silas felt a deep bass rumble in his chest and he grew queasy from the sensation. He realized that the commanding voice had touched his mind directly, putting the words in his head. He had not heard the voice—how could he have? To hear the true voice of such a creature of power would have obliterated him body and soul. His stomach roiled at the wrongness of it. "Spill his blood! Complete the ritual! Tear down the barrier!" The hands with far too many fingers pushed at the portal and the portal distorted as if seen through a lens. The cultists advanced on Silas, eager to do the Glutton's bidding.

Silas summoned a burst of lightning and it left a fist-sized, charred hole through the chest of one cultist. The confines were close and the cultists would not give him enough time to start another spell. He swung his staff towards another two but they merely stepped out of its arc and grabbed it before Silas could recover but it bought him space. Just as he moved to try another spell, a cultist knocked him to the floor in a bone-crushing hug. The leader loomed over him, smiling as she raised the knife to plunge it into Silas's chest. Seeing no other way to resist or escape, Silas closed his eyes, unwilling to watch the satisfaction on her face before he died. And then he heard a familiar yowl followed by a scream of pain and frustration.

Cautiously Silas opened an eye to find that the cult leader was no longer standing over him as Bundersnoot was busy clawing chunks out of her face. Her orders were muffled but the remaining cultists tried to get Bundersnoot off of her, which only resulted in Bundersnoot sinking his claws deeper into her flesh. It seemed the cultists were about to give it another go when Bundersnoot leaped from the leader's face and twisted through the legs of the other cultists before disappearing.

"Never mind the cat!" the voice of the Glutton rumbled. "Finish the ritual! Quickly! The planets are becoming unaligned!"

"Where's the knife?" the leader asked, but the cultists looked around in confusion. "Well where is it? It didn't just disappear into thin air!" They scrambled to search the sanctum, trying to find the obsidian blade. Silas smiled to himself.

"What are you smiling at?" the man pinning Silas asked.

"Ah, just a joke I heard about a cat," Silas replied. "It wasn't very funny. I'd tell it to you, but I think you don't really have the time for that." Already the portal was beginning to shrink. The limbs clawed desperately at its aperture but could not cross its threshold.

"Where is the sacrifice?!" the Glutton demanded. "Why have you betrayed me?"

"My lord," the cult leader got down on her knees, "I swear, this is no betrayal. I beg mercy. We were foiled."

"Foiled?! You told me all was in motion and you could not be stopped! Your enemies had been laid low! And now you give me sniveling excuses?"

"Mercy, my lord, mercy!" the cult leader prostrated herself before the portal that was rapidly diminishing.

"Failure comes with consequences." The Glutton said, and the cult leader screamed. Her body twisted unnaturally like a rag being wrung of its water, but Silas did not hear any bones break. The leader's scream was cut off as her body began to shrink, slowly but steadily diminishing to the size of a child, then a doll. "Let this be a lesson to you all," the Glutton said. The portal was so small now that Silas could have covered it with the palm of his hand. "In a thousand years' time, the planets will align once more and shall herald the coming of I, Yamlur'xex, the Great Glutton Whom…"

The portal abruptly shut and Silas felt his ears pop. The Glutton's speech had been interrupted and whatever means they had used to communicate with the mortal world had been severed, the magic of the ritual evaporating like morning mist. "We may have lost our window," the man pinning Silas growled, "but we can still make you pay."

"I think not," Lady Gavreau confidently strode into the room and placed the tip of her sword underneath the man's chin. Whatever spell that had concealed the sanctum from Gavreau and her warriors had died with the cult's leader. "Release my wizard." The bruiser raised his hands above his head and stepped away from Silas. Lady Gavreau's retainers rounded up the rest of the cultists and began marching them out of the sanctum.

"*Your* wizard?" Silas asked, pushing himself up from the floor. "I merely agreed to help save the world."

"I can still let them beat you to within an inch of your life. I may do so myself."

Silas sighed and bowed. "Yes, m'lady. Thank you for your timely rescue. I am eternally grateful."

"Better." Lady Gavreau sheathed her sword and looked at the remains of the cult leader on the floor. "What in the name of the Empress is *that*?" Lady Gavreau bent down and picked it up in her hand to examine it. "It looks like a doll of Eugénie Larousse."

"If you say it looks like Lady Larousse then I suspect that—is what *remains* of Lady Larousse." Gavreau dropped the doll to the floor and wiped her hand on her trouser leg. "Oh, curse me for a fool, the child!" Silas rushed to the altar, forcing the manacles open with a well-practiced cantrip. He knelt and murmured a spell, his hands glowing with a soothing pale blue light. He waved his hands over the child, running from head to foot, eyes closed in concentration. "There's no physical damage but their mind,—gods above," Silas sat back and looked around the inner sanctum for his familiar. "Bundersnoot? Bundersnoot where are you?"

There was a muffled statement and Bundersnoot reappeared from where he'd been hiding, the obsidian dagger clutched in his mouth, which he placed on the floor. "Blech, tastes abominable. What do you need, Silas?"

Silas pointed to the sleeping child. Without a word Bundersnoot jumped into the child's lap, circled once and then settled down and began purring loudly. Unconsciously, the child started stroking Bundersnoot's fur. "Hopefully Bundersnoot will help heal the mental wound," Silas explained. "Cats are quite good at this sort of thing." Silas reached out and gave Bundersnoot a few rubs as well, focusing on just breathing for the moment.

Lady Gavreau kicked what was left of Lady Larousse with her boot and sheathed her weapons. "Overall I'd say it was a good night's work. A cult demolished and a rival eliminated."

"And the world saved," Silas said.

"I don't know about saving the world," Lady Gavreau said. It was clear the horrors and urgency of the night were already slipping from her mind. "These were some debauched aristocrats who let their fun go a little too far. And it would be such a shame if the level of their depravity came to public knowledge." She smiled but Silas merely looked away, unable to forget the impossible things that he alone had seen.

* * *

"For exceptional services to the Family Gavreau, we give Master Silas our eternal gratitude and hope that this matter need never be discussed again." Silas put down the brief note, signed with Lady Gavreau's own mark, which had arrived with a fat purse of silver. It was probably a good thing she didn't mention him when she made her bid for power. The last thing he needed or wanted was to get further enmeshed in Elade-voc's politics. Bundersnoot padded into the room and Silas looked up. "How's the waif?" he asked.

"They're still sleeping for now. I'll check back in an hour to see if the terrors come back but they've had considerable improvement over the past week. How's your research going?"

Silas looked at Toquer's manuscript. "Unfruitful. You know, I thought after so many decades of adventuring I had amassed enough knowledge I could just settle down and never leave Elade-voc ever again. But I suspect we need to go out on the road again."

"Where do you think we need to go?"

"For now we need to go meet Jarl Brynjar up by Tallpines. I need to poke around his library and see if I can get some answers. After that, who knows where we'll end up going?"

About the Author

Writer, historian, ferroequinologist, numismatist, polymath. These and other fancy words can all be applied to Kalpar with varying degrees of accuracy. Kalpar is the pen-name of B.A. Klapper, a born and raised Cincinnatian who lives there to this day with their loving and supportive spouse.